GUARDIANS
of GA'HOOLE
THE LEGENDS

The Coming of Hoole

ENJOY ALL OF THE BOOKS IN
THE GUARDIANS *of* GA'HOOLE SERIES!

Beyond the Beyond

Shadow Forest

Silverveil

Kingdoms
of S'yrthghar

The Barrens

Unknown
Forest

The Canyonlands

N

Broken Talon Point

Kingdoms of
N'yrthghar

eninsula
f the
pirit Woods

Ice
Narrows

Sea of S'yrthghar

Cape
Glaux

The Beaks

Forest
of Tyto

esert

✳ Soren's Hollow

River Hoole

"Where there are legends, there can be hope. Where there are legends, there can be dreams of knightly owls, from a kingdom called Ga'Hoole, who will rise each night into the blackness and perform noble deeds. Owls who speak no words but true ones. Owls whose only purpose is to right all wrongs, to make strong the weak, mend the broken, vanquish the proud, and make powerless those who abuse the frail. With hearts sublime, they take flight..."

GUARDIANS
of GA'HOOLE
THE LEGENDS

BOOK TEN

The Coming of Hoole

BY KATHRYN LASKY

SCHOLASTIC INC.

New York Toronto London Auckland Sydney
Mexico City New Delhi Hong Kong Buenos Aires

No part of this publication may be reproduced, or stored in a retrieval system, or transmitted in any form or by any means, electronic, mechanical, photocopying, recording, or otherwise, without written permission of the publisher. For information regarding permission, write to Scholastic Inc., Attention: Permissions Department, 557 Broadway, New York, NY 10012.

ISBN 0-439-79569-9

Text copyright © 2006 by Kathryn Lasky.

Illustrations copyright © 2006 by Scholastic Inc. All rights reserved. Published by Scholastic Inc. SCHOLASTIC and associated logos are trademarks and/or registered trademarks of Scholastic Inc.

Design by Steve Scott.

12 11 10 9 8 7 6 5 4 3   6 7 8 9 10 11/0

Printed in the U.S.A.   40

First printing, July 2006

Kingdoms of N'yrthghar

N

H'rathghar
Mountains

Birthplace of
Hoole

Bitter
Sea

Firth
of Fangs

Kiel Bay

Stormfast
Island

H'rathghar
Glacier

Bay of
Fangs

The
Tridents

Hock

Everwinter
Sea

Ice Talons

Elsemere
Island

Ice Cliff Palace

Ice
Narrows

Ice Dagger

Dark Fowl Island

Kingdoms of
S'yrthghar

Contents

Prologue

Octavia, the pudgy, elderly, blind nest-maid snake, slithered out onto the branch outside her old master's hollow. "Look. I might be blind, but I know that you've been out there all morning. Why aren't you in your hollows sleeping?" She wagged her head at the three owls — Gylfie the tiny Elf Owl, Twilight the Great Gray, and Digger the Burrowing Owl. Together with Soren, a Barn Owl, they were known as "the Band," and they had been waiting since dawn for Soren to emerge from Ezylryb's hollow. Octavia coiled up as a Spotted Owl alighted on the branch. "Oh, and now Otulissa! What are you doing here?"

"The same thing they are doing." Otulissa tipped her head toward the Band. "Waiting for Soren to come out. He's been in there reading for days now!"

Suddenly, two owls stuck their heads out from the hollow. "What's this all about?" It was Soren and his nephew, Coryn, the new king of the Great Ga'Hoole Tree.

"It's about us, Soren." Otulissa stepped forward. It might appear that Otulissa was somewhat bold in her approach to the king and his closest advisor, and also somewhat lacking in the deference due Coryn, but he didn't seem to mind. After all, Otulissa had known him before any of the others of the tree. It was she who had found him in the Beyond after he had fled from his evil mother, Nyra, and the Pure Ones. It was Otulissa who had taught him how to catch coals. It had taken him about one minute to master that skill. She had not taught him, however, how to retrieve the Ember of Hoole. He did that by sheer instinct.

"What is it, Otulissa?" Coryn asked.

"We want to hear the legends, too. We want to read them with you."

Gylfie turned to Digger and whispered, "I thought it was just going to be us? How did she horn in on it?"

"You know Otulissa," Digger said with resignation.

"Look, Soren," Otulissa continued, "I am the one responsible for teaching the legends and the cantos to the young'uns here at the tree. I am the ryb for Ga'Hoology, which includes the natural history of the tree and its owl history."

Soren looked at her. What she said made sense but it was really not for him to decide.

Coryn now turned to his uncle. Since he first arrived at the tree a few moon cycles ago, he knew immediately that Soren would be more than an uncle to him. He needed Soren as his mentor and guide, as he assumed this new and often confounding role of king.

"I think you should hear the legends, Otulissa. . . ." Coryn looked at Soren once more and then nodded at the other three owls. "And you as well. It is only fitting. But let me warn you that there is strong stuff in these legends. There are truths that will make your gizzards quake." He began to say more, but then hesitated. Let them find out for themselves, *he thought*. Let them find out the truth about my mother, Nyra. *Then he continued briskly.* "Come back at midnight." *Turning again to Soren, he said,* "Would it be possible to end night flight early and begin reading the second legend then?"

Soren blinked. *The young'un was not used to being king. He need not ask such a question. He could decide the matter himself.* Soren gave a barely perceptible nod. Coryn immediately sensed that it was his decision and yet he knew that the Band would always turn to Soren, who had been their leader for so long. Though he might be king, Coryn wanted to do nothing that could be judged as a lack of respect for Soren. Yet, at the same time, he himself must be king, must lead. It was a difficult line to fly. "Yes, we shall end early, and Soren will meet with you first to tell you what we learned in the first legend before we read the second."

And so just after midnight, the six owls gathered in the small, cramped, hidden chamber in the back of Ezylryb's hollow, where three ancient books — secret books — of the legends of Ga'Hoole had been kept for countless years. Ezylryb only revealed their existence on his deathbed when he had insisted that the new young king read them with his uncle Soren. They watched in silence with quivering gizzards as Soren brought forth the second book, a worn and dusty old tome. He blew the dust off the mouse-leather cover and wiped it with his wing. The once-dim gold letters now seemed to gleam, like ancient stars whose light finally has reached the earth: THE LEGENDS OF GA'HOOLE. Beneath this in smaller letters were the words: THE COMING OF HOOLE.

Soren opened the book, then looked up from the page. "Before I begin I should tell you that neither Coryn nor myself is sure who wrote this second volume of the legends."

CHAPTER ONE
The Tilt of Ice

In a distant icebound firthkin far up the Firth of Fangs as stars swirled in the longest night of the year, a lone Spotted Owl stood trembling on the frozen sea. She stood with scimitar raised, prepared to fight to the death. The owl was Siv, queen of the N'yrthghar. The ice scimitar was that of her dead mate, King H'rath. Facing her was Lord Arrin, her enemy. The ragged shadows of hagsfiends tore through the moon-blazed night above her. She had been brought to ground by them but she had escaped their dreadful fyngrot, the peculiar searing yellow light that streamed from their eyes. Over the vastness of time and despite their primitive brains these relic creatures had acquired strange powers, the powers of nachtmagen, a destructive evil magic. That Lord Arrin, a clan chieftain and one-time ally of King H'rath, had allied himself with these ghoulish birds was unthinkable. And yet it had happened.

Siv was fully prepared to die. But if she had to die, she

would die fighting. So with one wing crippled from her previous encounter with hagsfiends, she stood in a pool of moonlight with the raised scimitar. Lame and exhausted, she was threatening Lord Arrin!

"You can't be serious, milady," Lord Arrin said.

"I am deadly serious. Stand back."

"My dear."

"No 'my dears.'"

"All right, milady. Save yourself and save your young'un. Join us. You can be my consort, my queen, the queen of nachtmagen."

"I am already a queen. Queen of the N'yrthghar. I need no other court, no other kingdom."

Lord Arrin stepped forward on the ice and swept a ragged wing toward the half dozen hagsfiends who were now closing in on her from above. "But this is your court."

"Never." And in her gizzard at that second, Siv knew that somewhere in this vast kingdom an egg was beginning to crack and a chick would soon hatch. And that chick was hers. A prince, the rightful heir of the N'yrthghar, was about to be born, and she would do all in her power to protect him from Lord Arrin and his hagsfiends who so desperately craved to possess him and the power that would be his.

"I ask you again, milady. Has the egg hatched yet?"

Siv remained silent.

"Where is the egg right now?"

Still only silence.

The egg was with Grank, somewhere far from Siv, and though separated from it, she still felt a deep connection. Lord Arrin's questions began to blur in her mind. She was in another place. Yes, the egg was hatching now, just as the night grew even darker. A shadow began to pass over the moon. She saw Lord Arrin wilf slightly and heard the harsh whispers of the hagsfiends. Their fyngrot was being swallowed by an immense shade. They hovered in flight and then alighted on the field of sea ice. Their huge wings hung like dark rags on the gleaming white.

It is a magic greater than theirs, Siv thought, as the moon began to vanish and a thick darkness enveloped them. *And yet not magic at all. They will never understand it.* As the earth passed between the sun and the moon, an eclipse was beginning, and little by little the earth's shadow bit slices from the moon. Within a matter of seconds there would be no moon. *Just darkness, complete darkness,* Siv thought, *and that will be my chance.* But would her badly mangled wing be strong enough to let her escape?

At the exact moment of complete darkness when all had grown utterly quiet, there was an immense cracking noise, and then a roar.

"The moon's shell is breaking!" one hagsfiend screeched.

Idiots! Siv thought.

It was not the moon. It was the ice. Svenka's massive polar-bear head poked up through it. All became topsy-turvy as the ice began to tilt, and water suddenly flooded over the jagged edges, swamping the sheet of ice.

"Quick, Siv, on my back!" Svenka called.

Siv quickly hopped onto her old friend's back and nestled herself deep in the ruff of fur around her neck.

As Svenka swam away, Siv peeked through the fur and saw one hagsfiend slide, shrieking, into the water. No one would come to its aid. Despite all their powers, hagsfiends feared one thing: water from the sea. The salt water saturated their oil-less wings making flight almost impossible. Siv watched as the hagsfiends tried to take off from the madly tilting ice fragment that was now awash with seawater. Three managed. Two others, however, skidded into the ocean. There was a searing howl as a hag's port wing was grabbed by the water. Siv blinked to see more clearly who it was. Then silently prayed, *Glaux, may it be Ygryk! Let it be Ygryk!*

CHAPTER TWO

A Shadow King

Outside the hollow, the world darkened as the shadow of the earth slid across the moon, but inside the air seemed to vibrate with a new luminosity as the shimmering egg rocked violently, shuddered one last time, and then split wide open. Grank gasped. It was Grank who had rescued the egg and brought it to this lonely island in the middle of the Bitter Sea. His assistant, Theo, looked over his shoulder in awe as the tiny featherless blob flopped from the shell and then tumbled onto the puffs of down they had prepared for him. Tufts plucked from both their breasts. Theo peered at the fluffy white under-feathers and wondered how the down from two such different owls, for he was a Great Horned and Grank was a Spotted, could look so similar.

The chick's eyes were still sealed shut. His head seemed enormous in comparison to his body. He looked no more a prince than any other newly hatched chick. Grank leaned over and bent very close to the chick whose body was still throbbing from the exertions of hatching. "Welcome, little one. Welcome, Hoole." Grank thought he saw the head flinch. Then he detected a movement pulsing ever so slightly behind the eye slits. Then one eyelid popped open and a gleaming dark eye was revealed. It was dark, but not black like a Barn Owl's, and not yet the rich amber of a Spotted Owl. That would come later.

"Welcome, Hoole." Theo bent forward and spoke in a very soft voice. Grank had warned Theo never to call Hoole "prince." His identity must not be revealed to him until the time is right. *Besides,* Grank had thought, *better he think of himself as a simple lad. It will make him work harder as a student.*

"The worms! Theo, do we have the worms?" Grank asked anxiously.

"Of course, right here."

Theo fetched a worm and began to drop it by the little owl's head.

"Here, I'll take that," Grank said quickly. Taking it in his beak, he crouched down so that his shoulders and head were on the ground, then twisted his head as only an owl can, by flipping it nearly upside down so that the worm was almost touching Hoole's tiny beak. Speaking out of the side of his own beak, he coaxed the chick. "First worm, Hoole, this is your First Worm ceremony. May

Glaux bless you and make your gizzard strong." The little owl opened his beak and took the worm. "Atta boy!" Grank boomed. Hoole shuddered and nearly dropped the worm. "Oops, sorry, lad."

Grank had never felt so much excitement as when the chick had taken that worm right from his beak and swallowed it headfirst. Traditionally, owls ate all of their prey headfirst. Of course, it was hard to tell with a worm which end was the head. "The lad's a natural, an absolute natural."

A natural what? Theo wondered. *A natural eater?* But Theo did not begrudge his master's enthusiasm. Theo would never begrudge Grank anything. He had learned more from Grank than he had ever learned from anyone else. Indeed, Grank was the only owl to have ever paid much attention to Theo. It was from Grank, who knew the secrets of fire, that Theo had first learned the possibilities of shaping metal into objects. Theo had a gift for the art of blacksmithing that was quite incredible. Until then, no one in the entire owl world had ever heard of this art of forging metals. Theo would someday be called the first blacksmith. His inventions would have an impact on the owl kingdoms as no other invention in the history of owls.

Nothing grows as quickly as a baby owlet. One minute Hoole was having his First Worm ceremony, then the next his First Insect, and before it seemed possible, his First Meat-on-Bones! Owls were ceremonial creatures and took quite seriously the many occasions that marked the important passages in their lives.

He was always hungry, this owlet. It seemed to both Grank and Theo that they were constantly out hunting prey for the little critter. Grank honestly did not know what he would have done without Theo. The young Great Horned Owl had had to cut back drastically the time spent at his forge. Grank called out to him now, and Theo looked up from his work.

"Theo!"

"Yes, sir."

"Can you fetch us another field mouse?"

Theo sighed. How could the little fellow eat so much? This had to be his third field mouse this evening, and the moon wasn't even up yet.

"Maybe I'll try for a vole, Grank. That might fill him up."

"Oh, a vole! A vole! I want a vole!" Theo heard Hoole's little peeping voice. Then, the little bundle of fluff — for he had not yet shed his down — hopped out on the branch and called to Theo below. "Theo, will you really get me a vole?"

"I'll try, Hoole."

"Back up there, lad," Grank said. "We don't want you taking a tumble off this branch. Your down won't work for flying."

"When will my first flight feathers come in, Uncle Grank?"

"Not until your fluff falls out. Your first molt."

"When will that happen?"

"When you start to budge."

"Have I started yet?"

"No. You'd feel it."

"Maybe not, Uncle Grank. Take a look please, please!"

Grank sighed. "All right, now wave good-bye to Theo."

"Bye, Theo! Uncle Grank's going to see if I've started to budge. Maybe by the time you get back I will have a flight feather."

"Oh, my!" Grank sighed wearily.

CHAPTER THREE
Theo's Discovery

Theo's favorite hunting ground for finding voles was a patch in the very middle of the island where a large circle of birch trees grew. But as Theo approached, he sensed something different. And then he heard it — a strange chanting. He perched for several minutes behind the thick clusters of needles on an interior branch of a very bushy pine tree. Listening intently, he realized what it was he was hearing. *Great Glaux, it's the brothers! The Glauxian Brothers!*

For years, the Glauxian Brothers had lived in widely dispersed ice holes and caves on the H'rathghar glacier, but he supposed the fighting had gotten too intense there and they needed a retreat where they could be safely together. The brothers were renowned for their studious ways. When they were not chanting, they were studying or writing; when they were not studying or writing, they were silent — for the most part. They had taken vows of silence so they might contemplate more deeply the mysteries of the owl universe.

Theo's feelings about discovering them here on what he had come to think of as his and Grank's island were conflicting ones. Theo admired the brothers greatly, and at one time had considered becoming one. Like the brothers, Theo did not believe in war. Furthermore, the brothers believed that the curse of the hagsfiends had been visited upon the N'yrthghar because the owls of this Northern Kingdom had lost their faith in Glaux and in reason. They believed that this loss of faith and reason had created a tear, a rip in the very air of the owl universe, and it was through this tear that these creatures of rage, superstition, and nachtmagen had gained their evil powers. It had pained Theo greatly when Grank had asked him, begged him to make that first pair of battle claws. He had only done so because Grank had revealed to him that the egg, whose well-being he was charged with, was that of King H'rath and Queen Siv.

But now he felt a horrible tearing within him. He hated making those battle claws as much as he loved Grank — Grank, who had taught him so much. Yet he knew that he himself was not at all like Grank. *Am I not of a more contempletive nature? Am I not more like these brothers?*

And yet . . . Theo paused in his deliberations. *And yet, I am devoted to Grank and to dear little Hoole. How could I think of abandoning them for the brothers?*

But the thought would not leave him entirely. Not for a long time, he knew, and perhaps never. Still, he must get on with the business of hunting down a plump vole for Hoole, and he could not do it here near the chanting brothers. He must do nothing to betray his and Grank's and Hoole's presence on this same island. Although the brothers were no threat, Grank had been adamant. "No one must know we are here!" How many times had he said that? The N'yrthghar was vast, yet word traveled fast in the bird world. Grank would be distressed when he heard that the brothers had set up camp on this island. But they could not move. Not until Hoole learned to fly. And they would probably have to shut down their fires. There must be no trace of smoke coming from their end of the island. Of course, the brothers might have already spotted it, for all Theo knew. In any case, he would now have to go elsewhere for a vole.

"Hello there, little one!" Theo said as he flew into the hollow with a plump vole in his talons.

"Umm-yum! May I lick the blood first?"

"What do you say to Theo, Hoole?"

"Oh, thanks, thanks."

Grank stopped himself just before saying, "A prince must be gracious to both vassal and servant." It still wasn't safe to tell this chick his true heritage at this point. Nothing would be more dangerous.

"Hey, check my right shoulder, Theo. Do you think I've budged any since you've been gone?"

"I've only been gone a little while, Hoole. Nothing happens that quickly." Grank was observing Theo and could tell almost immediately that something was disturbing the young Great Horned Owl. He would wait until dawn when Hoole would fall into the thick sleep of a chick with a full belly and tightly packed gizzard. Then they could talk.

Hoole's little body gave a tremendous shake as the bones, fur, and teeth of the vole he had just eaten lurched their way down to the second stomach, his gizzard. A drowsy, beatific look crept into his eyes. He yawned widely and then nestled into the down of his sleeping nest. "Tell me one more time, Uncle Grank, when is the soonest you think I can fly?"

"I told you, young'un. It usually takes Spotted Owls at least forty-two days before they can fly after hatching out."

"How long ago did I hatch out?"

"Barely ten."

"So is ten a far way from forty-two?"

"Go to sleep, Hoole."

"But I don't understand what forty-two is exactly."

"I'll explain tomorrow at twilight when you wake up."

Finally, the little owl gave a huge yawn and fell sound asleep.

"So, we are no longer alone," Grank said wearily, and clamped his beak shut. The first streaks of the dawn had spilled into the dark hollow, suffusing it with a rosy cheerful warmth — except Grank was far from cheerful over this news. "Well, we certainly can't leave until Hoole can fly. That's at least a moon cycle away and even then his flight skills won't be good enough nor his wings strong enough to go far."

"Look, Grank, I don't want to sound like a fool but, really, think about it. Sooner or later someone was bound to come here. We should be thankful it's the Glauxian Brothers. They are owls of great devotion. They would never betray our secret. For Glaux's sake, they take vows of silence. And although they hate war, they also hate Lord Arrin. And they had great faith in King H'rath and Queen Siv. They would do nothing to endanger the heir."

"They must not know that he is the heir. Never! No one

must know that." Grank paused and thought a moment. "I know what you say is true, and I don't for one minute doubt their loyalty or their devotion. But you know as well as I do how word travels. They are bound to find us before we can get away, and even if we appear just what we are — two owls with an orphan chick — word will get around that there is a chick without a mum being tended on the island."

"The brothers will hardly ever leave the island. You know how they are. Too busy studying, meditating."

"'Hardly' is not never." Grank sighed again. "Well, I suppose the first thing we should do is damp down the fires in the forge. If they haven't spotted our smoke by now, they certainly will soon. So you better get on with that. Be sure to keep the embers healthy so we can take them wherever we'll be going and start the fires anew."

"Yes, sir," Theo said.

He flew down and began to damp the fires in the slot of the immense boulder that they had used as a forge. The slot, with its natural updraft and slightly slanting walls, had proven to be perfect for creating intensely hot fires for the increasingly refined metalwork with which Theo had been experimenting. But now as he shut down these fires, he wondered why he was protecting the coals. Grank said new fires in some new place. *But new fires for what? To make more battle claws?* Or perhaps they were just for Grank's firesight. Grank was a flame reader. He could see things in fires that no other birds could. Things that were happening elsewhere — or were yet to happen. Firesight was as valuable to Grank as any nachtmagen.

Once again, Theo began to think about the Glauxian Brothers and their quiet scholarly lives. It was said that the Glauxian Brothers had learned how to inscribe things on pieces of special ice known as issen bhago. But these "bhags," as they were called, were heavy to transport. So they had decided to transcribe the bhags into books with pages written on the cured hides of the small animals. So now, before eating, they skinned whatever rabbit or rat or mouse they ate. It was an odd diet not having the fur and the skin, but the brothers were accustomed to making sacrifices.

Theo thought of all this as he smothered the fires while carefully putting aside the live coals in small, specially forged iron boxes that would keep them hot.

And for the first time in the months since Grank had been on the island, smoke did not curl up into the air above the tree and the hollow where he lived.

"Inside, Hoole! Immediately!" Grank said.

"But I just got out here!" Hoole was perched on the tip

of a branch. "You promised, Uncle Grank, that today would be the day for branching. My first flight feathers, remember? At last I have budged them."

"Back in the hollow," Theo said sharply.

This stunned Hoole. They never spoke this way to him. What had he done wrong — already? All he ever thought about was flying and now it was to be his first time and they hadn't even let him out on a branch! He must have messed up. But how? He poked his beak out a tiny bit.

"In!" Grank hissed.

Hoole had caught a glimpse of something flying overhead. He heard a stirring in the thinner branches high in the tree. Was some owl actually landing here? *Incredible!* Except for Grank and Theo, he hadn't ever seen any other owls.

Of course, the damping down of the fires had been in vain. Theo had smothered the fires only three days before, and now a brother was arriving at their campsite.

CHAPTER FOUR
The Encounter

It was useless trying to conceal Hoole in the hollow. The Glauxian Brother, a Boreal Owl who called himself Brother Berwyck, was a burly jolly bird. Not only had he spotted Grank and Theo, but he had seen Hoole peeking out of the hollow.

"Now, that's a fine young lad. And just got your flight feathers, eh? Try any branching yet?"

"I was just about to." Disappointment flooded Hoole's eyes.

"Oh, and then I came along and spoiled all the fun. Well, why don't you give it a try, young'un."

It was hard not to like Berwyck and even harder to be suspicious of such a gregarious and glad-spirited owl. So after instructions from all three of them, Hoole began to branch. He stepped tentatively off the larger branch to a smaller one just below. Then another and another without the merest trace of hesitation. Soon, he was going for the wider-spaced branches, feeling with delight that split second when there was nothing but air between him and the ground.

"I say, you've got yourself a fine lad, there. Going to be a real flier, that son of yours."

Should I correct him? Grank thought. But before he could even think of a reply, Hoole said, "He's my uncle. Right, Uncle Grank?" This startled Grank for he had never told Hoole what had become of his parents or that he was not exactly his real uncle. He had always told him "just call me Uncle Grank." As far as Grank knew, Hoole had no real sense of what a mum or da was, or a son for that matter, as opposed to a nephew.

"Yes, that's right, Hoole. I am your uncle." Then he gave a quick look to Brother Berwyck and whispered, "Sad story."

"Oh, yes," Berwyck whispered back. "So many chicks have lost parents in this fool war."

Hoole was too busy trying the latest branching tricks to pay any attention to this grown-up talk.

While Hoole continued his branching practice under Theo's watchful eye, Grank and Berwyck talked. Berwyck told Grank that he had seen the smoke some days before but hadn't had time to come explore its source until now.

"Oh, yes . . . well, I keep some live coals about," Grank was explaining. "Harvested them from a forest fire in the Southern Kingdoms some time back."

"You collect coals, eh?" Berwyck responded with a puzzled look.

"Er . . . uh, yes, I do. Funny little habit I picked up. I find them amusing."

"Amusing?" Berwyck lifted the dark feather tufts above his eyes. "Curious."

"Yes, they are curious . . . or rather, I'm curious . . . er . . . uh . . . yes. I'm a bit . . ." Grank was no good in situations like this. And although it wasn't outright lying, he wasn't much of a fibber, either. He knew that this Boreal Owl was a fine and honest owl. He hated being devious with such a fellow.

"Well," Brother Berwyck said, "maybe someday you will visit us at our retreat at the other end of the island and show us some of your amusing coals. You know we are determined to establish our retreat as a center for learning. Indeed, curiosity, in the best sense of the word, is what we as brothers celebrate. Everyone thinks of us as rather dull creatures, no fun at all, so much time spent in silence. But it is a loud silence for our heads are always buzzing with questions about the natural world. Yes, indeed, we would be most curious about your preoccupation with coals and fire."

"Well, perhaps someday, but for now I've got my talons full with this young'un."

"Oh, yes. I can see that."

It did not take long for Hoole to learn how to fly. In fact, it took him a spectacularly short time. He had begun his branching practice in the fragile lavender twilight and by the time the moon rose into the blackness of the night, Hoole was flying. They had made a lovely First Flight ceremony for him. Theo had tracked down a plump rabbit that Hoole tore into with great gusto. The white spots around his beak as well as the spots on his breast were now all red with blood. It was the first time he had ever eaten rabbit and he loved it. The fur was much finer than that of mice or vole and tickled pleasantly on its course to his gizzard. They had sung the First Flight song and then, as was the custom, took the snowy puff of the rabbit's tail, which they had not eaten, and threaded it into Hoole's head feathers. He was then required to fly once around the tree and return. Hoole felt a little bit stupid with the rabbit tail on his head and wished it had been a mouse or better yet a fox tail that would have streamed out behind him. But he knew not to complain. Besides, he was simply too thrilled with this wonderful new sensation of flight. He felt as though he had stepped into another world. And, in fact, he had. He was part of the sky. As he sailed off into the moon-streaked night, he felt sorry for all those poor wingless creatures that were bound to the earth.

"Watch this, Uncle Grank! Watch, Theo!" Hoole carved a perfect turn above the forge where several embers now glowed and the first flames rose up since the fires had been dampened three nights before. There was no sense in quitting the fires now that Berwyck knew all about them and the "curiosity" of Grank.

It seemed to Grank and Theo that Hoole never wanted to quit flying. Night after night he practiced and strengthened his newly fledged wings with their lovely tawny-edged flight feathers. *Just like his mum's,* Grank thought wistfully and wondered where Siv was. Siv, mother of Hoole, wife of the late King H'rath, friend of his own youth, and yes, he must admit it, love of his life. He was happy that Hoole had not asked him anything more about "parents" after Berwyck had referred to him as Grank's son. In truth, Hoole was too intoxicated with his newfound powers to contemplate such questions. All the lad wanted to do was fly, fly, fly. And when Grank or Theo called him home to the hollow, as the dark of the night thinned into the gray of dawn, he would always say, "Please, just five more minutes." He had no idea what five minutes was exactly but it sounded like a good long time to skim across the silk of the night, to catch a bit of a rogue wind or a warm draft from the fires and soar upward in effortless flight. Oh, how he loved flying!

In addition to lessons in flying and hunting, there were other things of a less practical nature that Grank taught Hoole — less practical but certainly necessary for a young prince, even if that prince did not yet know that he was of royal blood. Grank began to give Hoole short lectures on the code of honor that Hoole's grandfather had established for noblemen and their squires and knights, on and off the battlefield.

"One never attacks outside the field of battle, Hoole, and one never attacks an unarmed owl."

Hoole nodded thoughtfully.

"An owl who violates this code violates himself in the end. He endangers those seeds of Ga' that reside in every owl's gizzard."

"I don't understand what Ga' is, Uncle Grank."

"Ga' is difficult to explain, my boy. But I shall try."

"Are they really seeds?"

"No, I don't believe so. And if they were, they would be so infinitesimally small, one could never see them even if one could look straight into a gizzard. Ga' means great spirit; a spirit that somehow contains not just all that is noble but all that is humble as well. It flourishes in very few owls."

"Only in owls?" Hoole asked.

"Yes, I believe so."

"Have you ever known an owl with Ga', Uncle Grank?"

Grank looked hard at Hoole. "Not yet, lad. It's very rare." But his eyes grew misty as if he were remembering something. Only to himself would Grank admit that yes, he had met an owl that he suspected had great Ga' and that owl was Siv, Hoole's mother.

Unbeknownst to either Grank or Theo, Hoole did not confine his flying to just the night or the closest trees. Often after the two older owls were sound asleep, Hoole would sneak out of the hollow. Then one day, when the sun was the highest in the sky and he was returning to the hollow, Hoole spied something in the flames that licked up from the forge. What was it? It was real but not real. He could feel it. He could almost see it dancing on the edges of the flames. His gizzard clinched and for the first time in his short life he realized that there was something he missed. Something he missed terribly! But what could it be? He lighted down and peered harder into the flames.

CHAPTER FIVE

Yearning

Siv watched Svenka playing with her two cubs, First and Second. Polar bears waited a long time to give their cubs real names. Svenka had explained the reason for this was that so often they died. Names made living creatures more lovable — or so the bears believed. Siv did not believe this for one minute. She had seen Svenka with her cubs almost since birth and knew that Svenka had always loved them, named or not named.

The cubs were using Svenka as a slide, slipping off her back into the water. This was how they learned to swim. "Look at me, Auntie!" One of them called out now just before she splashed into the water.

"No, watch me, Auntie," the other bellowed.

Siv looked at the cubs and their mother with such yearning in her gizzard she thought it would break. She knew that at this very time, her own chick must be learning how to fly, or perhaps he already knew how. And she had missed it! She hoped that Grank had given him a good First Flight ceremony. Then she chided herself immediately. *Of course he did. How could I ever doubt dear Grank?* She shook herself a bit. She didn't want to appear sad in front of Svenka's cubs. It was a bright sparkling day on the water. Spring was coming. The ice was beginning to clear and this made it safer for her, because hagsfiends would not come around when there was so much open water. Furthermore, she sensed that Lord Arrin did not travel far without his posse of hags surrounding him. But at the same time, the iceberg that had been her home for months now was melting, shrinking smaller with each day's sun. Soon she would have to look for a new refuge. If only she knew where her chick was. But even if she did know, would she dare to go? It simply would be too dangerous. Then again, she thought, what if she could find him? She knew it was a male. Grank had told her so. He had seen it with that special vision of his that could read light and fire. *Yes, what if I really do find him? Then what? I cannot reveal myself as his mother. It would be too dangerous.*

Once before, Siv had disguised herself as a gadfeather. But still that would not solve the problem of where her chick could be found. How could she find out?

That night as the cubs slept nestled in the deep fur of Svenka's underbelly, their mouths all milky from nursing,

Siv told Svenka of her growing yearning for her hatchling, her son.

"The problem is I don't know where in the N'yrthghar he is or might be."

"What makes you think he's even in the Northern Kingdoms?"

Siv blinked. She had never thought of this. But surely he was too young to fly out of the N'yrthghar and into the Southern Kingdoms. She paused in her thoughts. *Or the Beyond. Would Grank have actually taken the chick to the Beyond?* she wondered. It was his favorite place and he had a good friend there, a wonderful ally, the wolf Fengo. But it was so far away. And yes, she had to admit, so safe. Oh, if only she could read the shards of light, the flames of the fire as Grank could, she might then know where her son was.

"I must see him, Svenka."

"But if you don't know where he is, how will you know where to go?"

It always comes back to that question, Siv thought wearily. How could she find out where he was? Then an idea burst upon her. "I must clad myself as a gadfeather again. Who knows more about where every creature in this N'yrthghar is but gadfeathers?" She did not wait for Svenka to reply. "They fly constantly. They are everywhere, all over the kingdom. They see everything. They hear everything."

"But they are stingy with their information, Siv. I know that for a fact. Ask them about herring runs and they want payment for it — a tuft of my fur, a whisker, a tooth I might have shed. Greedy, they are."

A sly sparkle glinted from Siv's amber eyes. She cocked her head and looked at Svenka. Svenka was a quick study.

"Oh, no, Siv! Not you, too!"

"Just one little whisker, please, Svenka. And look at that fur ball Second coughed up this morning."

"That disgusting thing! You're welcome to it."

"Oh, Svenka, thank you! Thank you!"

"Don't thank me, thank Second. And yes, you can have a whisker. Step up and pluck it out yourself but be quick about it. I still don't feel good about any of this, Siv."

"I know. It's probably all foolishness."

Svenka's eyes glistened. "No, Siv, it's never foolish to love a child, even when you cannot see him. I do understand." Svenka took her enormous paw and ever so gently touched Siv's shoulder.

It did not take Siv long to collect a few more gad-featherish trinkets with which to adorn herself. She found a rather fine blue-black cormorant feather and a dried-up fragment of a fishtail and with Svenka's help wove them into her feathers. When they had finished, Siv stepped gingerly to the edge of the berg and looked down at her gaudy reflection in the clear still water. "Great Glaux, what a sight!"

"You certainly look less than regal. No one would mistake you for a queen."

"That's just the point," Siv replied.

"So you're ready to go?"

"Almost."

"What do you mean, almost? I told you that the gadfeathers always gather up at the mouth of the firthkin on that island this time of year. If you don't want to miss them you had better fly soon."

"There is one thing that I want to happen before I go," Siv said, looking straight and unblinkingly into Svenka's eyes. The polar bear was clearly puzzled.

"What is it, Siv?"

"I want you to name First and Second."

"You do?" Now Svenka was completed bewildered. "But why?"

"Because you love them dearly, as do I, and you are not going to love them any more or any less if they are named or unnamed. I think you owe it to them. They are fine cubs. They put up with my dreary ways. They are already calling me 'Auntie.' You heard them the other day when they were sliding down your back."

29

Svenka nodded, tears glistening in her eyes. Siv was right. The cubs deserved to have names of their own. "So we shall have to have a Naming ceremony," Siv said.

Svenka chuckled to herself. *Oh, these owls and their ceremonies!* Was it simply not enough to give them a name? No, it never was enough with owls, especially Siv. The polar bear remembered that when Siv's beloved servant, Myrrthe, had been slain by the hagsfiends, Siv had climbed atop Svenka's head holding a white feather of Myrrthe's and had sung a beautiful song into the night. She had told Svenka that this was part of what owls called the Final ceremony. When an owl died, a special song was composed and sung at this ceremony. The song celebrated the memory of the owl who had died and who had hopefully found glaumora, the heaven of owls. Now Svenka roused her sleepy milk-drunk cubs so the Naming ceremony might begin.

Second blinked her huge dark eyes. "Auntie, what did you do to yourself? You look so pretty!"

"Oh it's just for fun, really, dear."

"We're going to give you names now," Svenka said gently.

"Names? What are names?" First asked.

"They are what we call one another."

"But I'm First and she's Second."

"Yeah, and I want to be First for a change."

"But I don't want to be Second."

"Neither of you will be First or Second. You shall be Anka," Svenka said nodding at Second. "And you" — she turned to First — "shall be Rolf."

"Rolf!" Rolf said with great delight. "Rrrrrolf!" He growled his name now. "I like that."

"Ahhhhnka!" Anka opened her jaw wide and let the sound roll around in her mouth and throat. "Ahhhhnkaaaa."

"Now quiet, dears," Siv said as she climbed atop Svenka's head, "and I shall sing you the song we owls always sing at the Naming ceremony when we have chicks. I'll change it a bit so it will fit for you cubs.

In the mighty roiling waters
of this cold and icy sea,
may you swim 'neath Ursa's eyes
may you grow up strong and free.
May you be true to your nature,
swift in water and on land,
for you stand the tallest of the tall
in this white and icebound land.
The greatest of the great in stature
and in power,

there is nary a living thing a polar bear
cannot devour.

And like your mum be massive in matters of the heart.
Be of good cheer and loyal, dear Anka and dear Rolf.

Siv left at First Black and headed for the mouth of the firthkin where Svenka had told her the gadfeathers gathered each year as the time of the spring equinox approached.

CHAPTER SIX

A Gathering of Gadfeathers

She heard the strains of the ice harp as she approached the point on which throngs of gadfeathers had gathered. She was nervous, but she knew that gadfeathers did not pry. They were very close-beaked about who they were and where they had come from. It was part of their culture, the gadfeather way of life. All of them at sometime or another had left something they called home or family for whatever reason, and it was considered a grave transgression to ask a gadfeather about his or her personal history. Theirs was a journeying way of life. They considered themselves free of loyalty to any region or clan or hollow. The words "free" and "freedom" threaded through many of their songs. They mostly traveled alone or sometimes in small flocks, but these flocks changed constantly. So even though they were known to be rather solitary creatures like polar bears, they did gather several times a year to meet and sing. The gift for making song and lovely music was one thing that all gadfeathers seemed to have in common. Among the most musically gifted of the gadfeathers were the Snowy Owls. As Siv drew closer, she could clearly hear one of the Snowies singing to the beautiful liquid notes of the ice harp. It was a mournful, soul-searing song.

> *Fly away with me,*
> *give my loneliness a break.*
> *Fly away with me,*
> *so my heart will never ache.*
> *Fly away with me this night.*
> *Fly away with me,*
> *I'll find a feather for your ruff.*
> *Fly away with me till dawn.*
> *Fly away then we'll be gone.*
> *Hollows we shall leave behind,*
> *fly to places they'll never find.*
> *Fly away with me right now,*
> *I can't wait.*
> *Fly away with me,*
> *don't hesitate.*
> *I want to soar the smee hole drafts*
> *where the steam rises from the sea.*
> *I want to cross the mountain ridge,*
> *I want to see the other side.*

We'll preen each other in the moon's light.
Fly away with me.
We shall wake up in the snow,
go where the winds always blow.
Fly away with me!

"Lovely, ain't it?" A Whiskered Screech lighted down on the ice cliff where Siv had perched.

"Oh, yes," Siv replied. The song had awakened so much loneliness in her. How she missed her beloved H'rath and the chick she had never met, and now Svenka and the cubs. She had never felt lonelier in her life. It struck Siv as rather ironic that gadfeathers disdained the life of family and hollow yet sang so beautifully of loneliness. It was as if they craved companionship yet celebrated loneliness.

"Nothing like a Snowy for singing. They call her the Snow Rose." The Whiskered Screech nodded at the Snowy Owl who had just finished singing. "Hope she sings 'Sky of Tears.' Just wait'll you hear that one. Your gizzard will be in shreds."

That is the last thing I need, Siv thought, *my gizzard in shreds!* She had to be alert and pulled together and keen for anything she might hear — not just these aching songs.

She flew onto another perch. Here, gadfeathers were swooping through the air doing one of their jigs while a

Great Horned Owl belted out another song full of hurt and anger, bad weather, and teardrops that froze feathers.

Enough of this! thought Siv. She flew off to where a group of owls were picking over a pile of herring that some Fish Owls had delivered. She sidled up to a small clutch of gadfeathers who were busily eating and talking.

"They say the fighting's moved back to the H'rathghar glacier. Lord Arrin, you know."

"Yeah, the last of H'rath's guard tried holding him off."

"Well, if they've moved to the glacier, that'll free up the Firth of Fangs for a bit of sport flying this summer. Nothing like them smee holes up there."

"Yeah, but there be kraals, too."

Kraals, Siv thought. What exactly were kraals? She had heard King H'rath speak of them once. She had thought they were some kind of gadfeather, but these owls were speaking as if they were something else entirely.

"They say that old Screech who used to fly with us went kraal last summer."

"They be a nasty lot."

"I heard they were settling down somewhere on the glacier."

"Naw, you got it mixed up. It's them Glauxian Brothers who are on the glacier."

36

"No, Mac, them brothers picked up and flew off. Started a retreat somewhere, like the sisters have."

This was news to Siv. She knew for a fact that the brothers had lived in the scattered holes on the glacier. Indeed, the brothers had often visited the Glacier Palace during the periods when they were permitted to speak. Throughout the year the brothers kept long periods of silence. And even during the rest of the year, each day had certain hours in which they kept the rule of silence. They had always been welcome at the palace, for both Siv and H'rath had enjoyed them greatly. They were most learned owls, and it had been Siv's hope that if she and H'rath ever did have a chick, one of the brothers might be convinced to come and tutor it. She had often heard them speak of their longing to have a retreat, a place where they could all live together in what they called a community of learning instead of living scattered. They dreamed of starting a library in which they could keep records of all they had learned. So, it seemed at last they had done this.

"It's peaceful over there in the Bitter Sea. Hasn't been touched by the wars. That's probably where they've gone."

"Not much to fight for over there. Not like around here. I heard tell the hagsfiend Ygryk had been spotted not ten leagues from here."

Ygryk! Siv's gizzard froze. *Ygryk near here?* The thought was too terrible. She would have to be extra careful. She would need more gadfeatherish bits and pieces to tuck in. Nearby was a pile of reindeer moss. She had noticed one gadfeather had swathed some around her head, lending her a rakish air but also obscuring her face. She went to the pile and plucked some up and while arranging it, continued to listen to the two gadfeathers that had been talking.

"Bitter Sea never freezes up. You ain't gonna get Lord Arrin over there now that he's cozied up with the hags-fiends. Too much open water. Salt water. Odd how it be only salt water that gets them hagsfiends, and not rain-water so much."

"Lose their half-hags from the salt. Salt usually makes things melt. But when it gets mixed with that poison of the half-hags it makes them freeze up, then the feathers of the hagsfiends start to freeze and down they go. No oil in their feathers, either, like the rest of us, which helps us shed salt water."

The terrible half-hags! Siv remembered them vividly. They had never reached her for she had successfully blocked the fyngrot. However, she would never forget the image of them swarming over her mate as he fought Lord Arrin. Nevertheless, H'rath had fought on as the poison coursed through his hollow bones, dissolving them and then flooding into his bloodstream. But it had been Lord Arrin who had delivered the fatal blow. And then the hagsfiend Penryck had sliced off H'rath's head, jammed it onto his ice sword, and swooped off into the night. The hagsfiends were known for their ghoulish ritualistic ways of murder. Siv clamped her eyes tightly shut against this rush of memories.

"*'Too much open water*'!" The words rang now in Siv's brain. Her gizzard tingled. Why had she never thought of this before? The Bitter Sea would be the perfect place for Grank to have taken the egg on that night when they had been attacked by the hagsfiends in the Ice Cliff Palace. She would go there immediately!

CHAPTER SEVEN

A Deadly Plan

As Siv plied her way west toward the Bitter Sea against a headwind that made her barely healed port wing throb with pain, Lord Arrin was meeting with his band of hagsfiends and commander owls in a cave on the H'rathghar glacier. There were twenty owls with the rank of commander, each of whom had a company of no less than ten owls. Every one of the twenty units had a hagsfiend attached to it. And there were some units composed entirely of hagsfiends. The cave was crowded with the twenty commanders and six hagsfiend captains. And on each hagsfiend, unseen, lurked scores of miniscule half-hags. They lived in the interstices and narrow, slotted spaces between the hagsfiends' feathers. It was from these nearly invisible refuges that the half-hags would dart out in battle with their poisonous loads. The hagsfiends themselves had built up a strong immunity to the poison. If one were to look closely, its feathers, even while the hagsfiend was resting, would appear to be moving slightly as if stirred by the most delicate wind. But it was actually the half-hags. Like ants in an anthill, they went about their business constantly and their business was to feed off the small lice and other tiny vermin that lodged in their hosts' wings. Perched in the shadows behind Lord Arrin was his closest confidant, Penryck, who was the captain of one of the hagsfiend units. Penryck who was also known as the Sklardrog, which in Krakish means sky dragon. He was a bold hag full of wit and magic, and Lord Arrin had come to rely on him more and more as the war had turned in his favor. The Glacier Palace of the H'rathghar was now within their reach. They would lay siege to it by summer's end, before the katabatic winds started to blow.

But what was a palace without a queen? Lord Arrin needed Siv, and he needed the chick who must have hatched by now, but where were they? Where was this chick who might have greater powers than any of them could imagine? Luckily for Lord Arrin, few had imagined these powers. It was Penryck who had first suggested to him that the chick might have a special energy. They had only caught a glimpse of the egg as Siv and her servant, Myrrthe, had fled from the Glacier Palace when King H'rath had been killed. The egg had possessed a peculiar luminosity, which had resisted the fyngrot. The searing yellow light had slipped off the egg, simply melted away like ice crystals in the heat of the sun. Indeed, the egg had grown even more radiant.

And had this radiance in some way rubbed off on Siv? Was that how she had resisted the fyngrot? It was quite extraordinary. She had seemed impervious to the yellow glare. This had both fascinated and frightened the hags-fiends. They imagined that both Siv — and especially her chick — had untapped magic. And if there was any magic greater than their own in the N'yrthghar, the hagsfiends lusted for it. They were the rightful heirs of nachtmagen! No others but the hagsfiends could possess it.

But magic was not all. They needed an alliance with a powerful owl like Lord Arrin. Despite their nachtmagen, they still were peculiarly vulnerable to seawater. Thus, there were only limited regions that they could control, but with Lord Arrin this problem was solved. Solved, that was, as long as he himself did not become too haggish through association. That is why he desperately craved Siv for his mate. She who could resist the fyngrot, would thwart those haggish tendencies, would make him immune to that one vulnerability he had learned by Pleek's example.

The lesson of Lord Pleek and Ygryk was a harsh one. For as soon as Pleek had taken Ygryk as a mate, he had begun to acquire certain haggish aspects and was now beginning to fear open water. The union between the Great Horned and the hagsfiend had proved to be a chickless one. Eggs were laid but they never developed. After a few days, they shriveled up into gray, hard, misshapen spheres. Nonetheless, Lord Arrin and Penryck had discussed how they might best use Pleek and Ygryk in obtaining Siv's chick. Ygryk longed for a chick of her own. She was desperate, so desperate that she was willing to fly over open water to get one if need be. She was obsessed. It had been Ygryk who had actually found Siv on the iceberg in the firthkin.

And it was Ygryk who had just informed Penryck that Siv had left the iceberg. Penryck stepped out of the shadows now. "Lord Arrin, I have just received news from Ygryk that Queen Siv has left the iceberg in the firthkin."

"Left? She has left?" Lord Arrin was aghast. "What now? How will we ever find the chick?"

Penryck stepped closer to Lord Arrin and, leaning in to him, whispered something in his ear slit. Lord Arrin cringed. The stench of these hagsfiends was overpowering. He wondered if one ever became accustomed to it.

But he was soon distracted from such trivialities as he listened to the hagsfiend's whispers.

"It is as I always thought, my lord. The egg was never there with Siv. The chick did not hatch at the firthkin, and if it did it would have been much too young to fly — certainly not against those spring winds of the firthkin. If Siv left, she must have been alone."

Lord Arrin blinked. *He's right. Penryck is right.* "But what now, Penryck?"

"Don't you see, Lord Arrin, it is a blessing." It was very odd hearing a hagsfiend say a word like "blessing." A blessing was associated with Glaux, with faith, but never with magic. The word sounded curious from the beak of a hagsfiend, something like the krakish word for blood, "bleshka."

"How so?" Lord Arrin asked.

"A mother yearns for her chick. If we find her, we can follow her. She will lead us right to the chick."

"Aaaah." Lord Arrin blinked. His amber eyes glowed with this sudden realization.

Penryck wondered yet again how stupid these owls were. Not only did they have no magic but they, who thought that hagsfiends brains were primitive, had their own unique ignorance. Lord Arrin might imagine that he, Penryck, was working for him, but in truth it was quite the reverse. Penryck himself had a grand scheme for domination, and if they could seize the chick . . . well . . . the world would be Penryck's and he would not be just king of the N'yrthghar but the god of the nachtmagen universe.

The other owls and hagsfiends whispered among themselves as Lord Arrin and Penryck continued to confer.

"We need the best trackers," Lord Arrin was saying in a low voice.

"Well, we know who that is!" Penryck churred. But it was not the soft gentle laughter of owls. Instead, it sounded rather like ice fracturing.

"Ygryk! How convenient."

Penryck nodded.

"Invite her and Pleek to the war room," Lord Arrin said, and then paused. "Of course, we won't let Ygryk actually keep the chick. She could be its foster mother, nanny, nursemaid, perhaps."

Penryck shook his head. "No, that will never do. She will want to possess the chick entirely."

Lord Arrin blinked. "Well then, there is only one choice."

Penryck nodded.

"She will be slain as soon as she leads us to the chick."

"Precisely," Penryck replied.

"And we know who our best assassin is — Ullryck,"
Lord Arrin said. He then churred. *This, indeed, is a good plan,*
he thought to himself. "Yes, yes, a good plan. Send for
Ygryk and Pleek right now!"

Ygryk and Pleek followed Penryck as they flew
through a tangled web of ice tunnels under the H'rathghar
glacier. Their gizzards were tight. Their hearts beat rapidly. Never before had they been asked into this innermost
sanctum where Lord Arrin had plotted and strategized
against the H'rathian owls of the king. *We are coming up in
the world,* Pleek thought. How they had made fun of him.
No, worse. When he had first taken Ygryk as a mate, they
all had sneered and treated him as if he were splat from a
wet pooper of a bird, a seagull. But look at him now — and
look at Ygryk — both of them flying toward the war
room to be included in a high-level meeting.

Lord Arrin began at once. "We have invited you here
to perform a special mission."

"Your word is our command." Pleek dipped his head
obsequiously.

"Ygryk, I understand that because of your superb vigi-
lance you have just discovered that Siv has fled the
iceberg."

46

"Yes, my lord." Her voice creaked in the manner of those hagsfiends whose ancestors were said to have emerged from the smee holes that dotted the N'yrthghar. Somehow the heat or the steam from the holes and had given their voices an odd inflection.

"I know that it is difficult for you hagsfiends with your . . ." He hesitated as if searching for the proper word.

Don't you dare say "primitive," Penryck silently cursed.

". . . With your unusual brains and thinking processes to master the art of reason, but I have deduced that it would be most logical at this time for Siv to set out in search of her chick."

No credit for me, of course! Penryck thought.

"Therefore," Lord Arrin continued, "my proposition is simple. Ygryk, you are a superior tracker and you, Pleek, have learned well from this good mate of yours."

At last, Pleek thought, *someone understands what a jewel my Ygryk truly is!*

"I want Siv as my queen," Lord Arrin went on. "You want a child. You get me my queen and her chick. I'll keep the queen and you keep the chick."

Pleek and Ygryk were overwhelmed. They slid from the ice shards they had been perched on and bent their legs so deeply that their talons skidded out from under them and their beaks dug into the ice. "Merciful and all wise Lord Arrin," Pleek began, "how shall we ever thank you for this?"

Lord Arrin looked down at them groveling at the tips of his talons. "Oh, I'm sure we will find a way." He blinked and the amber in his eyes cast golden shadows on the ice. He paused. "Now, you are dismissed."

The Great Horned and the hagsfiend, bowing and scraping, backed out of the war room. Then Lord Arrin turned to Penryck. "Send for Ullryck. She's got no longings for chicks? No notions of mothering?"

"Not our Ullryck, sir. 'Twas said that her ancestors came from the deepest smee hole in the N'yrthghar, one that went straight down to hagsmire."

"Perfect, then, for this job. Give her flight instructions immediately. She'll need two burly fighters with her for the trip back. They're not to set off until Pleek and Ygryk are a few leagues out. Her half-hags should be able to pick up their scent. Give her a cover story if they discover her; just say that I felt they might need some backup if things got rough."

"Yes, my lord."

"My lord?" Lord Arrin blinked at Penryck with a hint of contempt in his amber eyes.

Penryck was momentarily confused. *Surely he does not want me to call him 'Your Majesty' yet! Not yet!*

Penryck dipped his head. His shaggy black feathers scraped the ice. "Your Majesty?" At the very core of the word was a quaver of doubt. But if Lord Arrin noticed he chose to ignore it.

Fool! thought Penryck.

CHAPTER EIGHT
The Passion of Ygryk

Pleek regarded his mate, Ygryk, who flew a good distance ahead of him, her head sweeping in a wide arc as she sniffed the air. How stunned his family had been when he had chosen a hagsfiend for his mate. "A disgrace," they had hooted. "Outrageous!" screeched an elderly aunt. But where they saw filth, he saw a dark purity. Where they smelled the stench of crow, he experienced only the heady scent of nachtmagen. She was magnificent and powerful. The half-hags that flew in the fringes of her primaries served her well because she commanded them so expertly. And it was for this reason she was one of the finest trackers in the N'yrthghar. These tiny poisonous half-hags darted out from beneath the edges of her flight wings on short forays to detect clues from the long-vanished flight paths of owls. It might have been hours since an owl had passed through a patch of sky but a half-hag could sense the most minute vestiges in an air current disturbed by the wings of a particular owl. It might be anything —

a tiny filament of down still spinning in a swirling eddy, the scent of a pellet yarped in flight. Nothing was too small, too insignificant, for these tiny poisonous creatures to detect. And their obedience to Ygryk was unparalleled, unequivocal, and beyond that of any other half-hags. This made Ygryk the best tracker.

They knew exactly what they were looking for. As soon as Lord Arrin had given them their flight orders, Pleek had returned to the iceberg where Siv had nested. They waited until Svenka and her cubs were off fishing and picked up a feather Siv had shed. This was enough to provide the half-hags with her scent. Furthermore, Ygryk had explained to them, in that odd language that was used only by hagsfiends to communicate with their half-hags, how Siv's flight marks would differ; because of her damaged port wing, she would be favoring her starboard wing. Therefore the air she passed through would be unevenly disturbed.

The half-hags' first clue had been picked up in a maverick eddy that had spun off an air stream coming off the island of Dark Fowl.

"Two points north of east," Ygryk called to her mate. She flipped her head back to make sure he was following. How incredible it seemed to her that a true owl had chosen her for his mate. How seldom this happened. She felt so proud. And Ygryk's family was as proud as Pleek's was ashamed. The only problem was that they had been unable to have offspring. Only a few of these rare unions provided offspring, and for most hagsfiends it was not a problem. But for Ygryk it was. Deep within her she had a longing that was different from anything she had ever known. She adored anything young and vulnerable. Now, many hagsfiends were fascinated by the innocence of chicks or cubs or pups, but it was not a loving fascination. Quite the reverse. They enjoyed killing the defenseless and the innocent. The blood of innocents was a tonic on which they thrived. They had even been known to eat their own young. Ygryk, too, had bloodied her beak countless times on young polar bear cubs left while their mothers went hunting. She had swooped down on a fox's kit that had scampered from its den. And nothing was more delightful than a nest full of soft newborn bunnies. The pathetic mewlings of the mother before Ygryk would rip out its throat, the wide-eyed disbelief of those babies as she slowly ate them one by one, too stupefied even to run. But this fascination and thrill of power over the innocent had turned to something else when she had met Pleek and had thought of a chick of her own — half-owl, half-hagsfiend — a dear little creature. She had imagined it for so long. The chick would have, of course, two dark brown tufts that rose on top of its head, just like Pleek's. And she pictured its plumage mostly black but shot through with some of the grays and tans of a Great Horned. Its eyes would be the lovely amber of Pleek's. When she'd begun to realize that this was not going to happen, that there would be no chick, she tried to remember some old nachtmagen spells that she had heard about from an ancient crone of a hag who lived deep in the Ice Narrows. She had visited the hag. Kreeth was her name, and Ygyrk had looked at some of the peculiar birds Kreeth had produced from her experiments with puffins, which were prevalent in the region. Some had called the resulting birds monstrosities, but Ygryk found them quite charming.

"It can de done," Kreeth had told her. "Better not to get an egg though. Better to get a hatchling or even a young owlet just learning to fly. Then if you set your half-hags around it and say the first spell, it will make the chick resistant to the poison. After that you must move on to the second spell."

"And what is that?" Ygryk asked.

Kreeth waited to reply, then spoke. "You won't like it, but it must be done. You must trust the spell. It is called the nacht blucken."

"What is it? I'll do anything."

Kreeth had looked at her carefully. Yes, she believed this desperate hagsfiend would do anything. The passion was there. "You must pluck out one of its eyes," Kreeth said.

"What?"

"You heard me. You must pluck out one of its eyes."

"But how will it see to fly?"

"Fear not. It will grow another eye very quickly but where the eye was, the powers of the fyngrot will enter."

"It will have fyngrot even though it started as a simple owl?" Ygyrk was stunned.

"There is nothing simple about an owl. Nothing at all. And if you get a special owl, one of great lineage and powerful ancestors, you will have created a most magnificent creature."

When Ygyrk had told Pleek about this, their desire to find a chick that they could make their own became an obsession for both of them. And then when they had heard that Siv had laid an egg, the obsession became an all-encompassing passion. To steal the egg of King H'rath and Queen Siv, and when it hatched to ensnare that chick into the web of spells she had learned from Kreeth — why they dared not even imagine the possibilities! Their powers would exceed those of any living thing not just in the N'yrthghar but in the entire universe of owls, no, of all creatures.

A half-hag flew up to Ygryk and reported that a thread of down from the target owl had been detected amidst uneven air currents leading to the region just south of the Bitter Sea, near the Ice Dagger.

Ice Dagger! Bitter Sea! thought Ygryk. Open water! But nothing would stop her. Her passion, a mere spark in the beginning, was now raging inside her like a fire. She would fly through any wind, any storm, over any sea! The heat of her passion would keep her dry. She would become as impervious to seawater as hagsfiends were to the poison of their half-hags. She would get this chick. She would be a mother. A *mother*! The word screamed in her head. And if she had had a true gizzard it might have shattered from the tumult of her feelings.

Some time earlier, Siv had lifted off from the Ice Dagger where she had taken a good long rest. Her wing felt much restored and, with the wind dying, she hoped to reach the Bitter Sea by moonrise. If, indeed, she would even see the moon tonight. There was a thick cloud cover, which she blessed. Her disguise was good but still, as she flew, she took care to bury herself deep within any clouds. She tried to imagine what her chick might look like. Would he have her eyes or maybe H'rath's, the amber sparkling with bright glints of gold? Would he have inherited her gift for verse? There were so many things to imagine with this chick. The hardest, of course, was to picture herself holding back, not rushing up to preen him, but concealing her own identity. But conceal she would. She was firm in her gizzard on this point. She would do nothing to endanger his life. When she found him — if she found him — she would observe him from afar and she would only approach him if Grank was not around, if he was alone. Grank knew her too well. He would recognize her instantly and although he would not betray who she was, it would make life more difficult for him and the last thing she wanted was to make anything difficult for Grank. She owed Grank if not her own life then that of her son. It suddenly struck Siv that for her there was no distinction between the two of them: Her life was inextricably entwined with that of her chick. There was, from her point of view, no separation. If he died, she would die. She knew this as well as she had ever known anything. But if she died, she felt deep within her gizzard that he would go on. And that was really all that mattered.

Through a sudden patchy thinness in the clouds, the retreat of the Glauxian Sisters came into view. Her cousin Rorkna was the abbess of the sisters. How she would love to light down there for a visit. It had been so long since she had seen her. But it would not do. There must not be a whisper of her presence in this region even if she was disguised as a gadfeather.

She thought now about her visit at the gathering of gadfeathers. She had actually found it rather pleasant. When she was young, she remembered her mother and aunts talking disdainfully of their slovenly undisciplined lives, their refusal to settle in with the rest of the owl communities, their desertion of their families, their rowdy ways and, of course, their reputations for stealing anything that wasn't embedded in strong ice. But she had found in them a certain gentleness and she had never heard anyone sing as beautifully as the Snow Rose. If she were still the reigning queen in the Glacier Palace she would have invited the Snow Rose to come and sing there. She thought of all that now. She thought of what lovely times there could have been. She would have grown old in the palace along with King H'rath. Perhaps they would have had more than one chick, and they might have watched them grow up and grow strong and become knights of the H'rathghar like their father and grandfathers. And there would have been evenings of song and feasting. And yet she was ready to trade all that now for just one glimpse of her son.

CHAPTER NINE
Facts of Life

Hoole had become fascinated with the fire in the forge and the image that he had spied at the edge of its flames. It made his gizzard clinch every time he saw it. Lately the image had moved from the edge of the flame to the center and had become larger. It appeared to be some sort of bird, but it was not flying like an owl. It seemed to limp through the air. And yet his gizzard yearned for it, yearned for something he could not quite see or know.

It was about this time that many questions began to fill Hoole's mind. And as close as he felt to both Grank and Theo, for some reason he hesitated asking them. Somehow he sensed that these questions might disturb them, especially Grank. Oftentimes, he had been on the brink of asking, and then would quickly decide against it. In many ways the questions were like the image that he saw in the fire. He knew something was there, but he did not recognize it. He did not know the words for it. And it was the same with the questions. They hovered at the edge of his mind and yet he did not have the words for them.

Brother Berwyck came to visit them often and although he frequently invited them to the retreat, Grank always found a reason to refuse. Grank did, however, permit Hoole to spend time with Berwyck. He knew that if Hoole were to rule he must be familiar with all kinds of owls, all species, and Boreal Owls were known for their tolerant and giving natures. He also knew that Brother Berwyck, like all of the Glauxian Brothers, was a scholarly owl. So there would be much Hoole could learn from him. Brother Berwyck himself seemed to understand that Grank was somewhat of a loner and respected his desire to remain aloof. Grank had never asked Berwyck not to tell his fellow Glauxian Brothers about them, but somehow Berwyck sensed that Grank would prefer it if he kept the knowledge of the two owls and their young charge to himself. Still he was made to feel welcome whenever he came to visit. Brother Berwyck had shown Hoole a cove that furrowed in from the Bitter Sea, which, in the springtime when the ice melted, was his favorite hunting ground. Oddly enough, the brother had a taste for fish even though he was not a Fish Owl. He had promised to teach Hoole how to fish, and although the young prince did not much care for the taste of fish, the sport of fishing seemed like it might be great fun.

It was a wonderful time now in the N'yrthghar, particularly in the region of the Bitter Sea. Grank often said it should be called the Sweet Sea at this time of year, for the earth unlocked, much of the snow melted, and even where it did not, wildflowers sprang up at the edge of drifts. There were bright little yellow stars called avalanche lilies and tiny pink blossoms named teardrops of Glaux. Fragrant herbs and wonderfully soft mosses grew everywhere. Game was plentiful, though a bit scrawny after moon cycle upon moon cycle of deep winter.

One lovely spring evening at the cove, Hoole was having his first fishing lesson as Berwyck coached him from an overhanging limb of an alder. "That's it, Hoole. You know when you do that downward spiral to break through the water, really lay those wings back close to your body. You want to be as a sleek and narrow as possible, like an ice blade slicing through the water."

Hoole felt the water divide as he hit it. Silvery bubbles streamed back from his head. It was as if he were racing through a starry liquid night. His third eyelids slipped into place to protect his eyes from the water and any debris, just as they did in foul-weather flying. A grummy swam by. It was strange but he knew exactly what that fish would do. Indeed, he almost felt like a fish himself. Observing how the creature swam, he realized that in many ways swimming was like flying, and water was like air. There were waves of water just as there were drafts of air one could ride. To turn, the fish had to rudder its tail just as Hoole had to do when flying, and was doing right now underwater while tracking the fish. Then he started backstroking with his wings, which were almost like the grummy's fins. At this particular moment, he felt himself become more fish than owl. Yet he still had his feathers, his talons. Suddenly, he knew this was the moment to snatch out with both talons. The fish was his! He burst through the surface of the water, the silver-blue grummy flopping about but firmly gripped in his talons. He deposited it at Berwyck's feet and looked up.

"Good job. You're a natural!"

Hoole hesitated.

"You know the rule, lad," Berwyck said. "You catch it, you eat it! We don't hunt for amusement!"

"Yes, Brother Berwyck."

"Give it a good thwack and put it out of its misery, or its misery will shortly become your misery. You don't want that critter flopping around inside you. They're scratchy, especially the tail when you swallow them alive."

Hoole gave it a good thwack, and the fish was instantly dead. He looked at it for a few seconds.

"Pretty, isn't it?" Berwyck said.

It was. In death, grummies turned all the colors of the rainbow. The silver and blue flushed into tints of rose and gold and purple and green. It was odd to think that death could have such beauty. Hoole blinked and gulped down the fish.

Somehow thinking about that question of death unleashed within him the other questions he had been wondering about for so long: questions not about death but about life.

"Berwyck," Hoole began slowly.

Berwyck looked at him intently. He sensed that something of great import was about to happen, that this incredibly bright young owl wanted to know something vital.

"Berwyck," Hoole began again. "How did I come to be?"

"To be?" Berwyck replied in a stunned voice. Although he had expected to be asked something important, he was astonished by the way Hoole put it.

"You were hatched, Hoole. You hatched out of the egg."

"But what was there before the egg? Who made the egg? Uncle Grank?"

"No, no. It's . . . er . . . well . . . it takes two owls to make an egg."

"Two. Well, who were the two?"

"Well, a male and a female."

"Male? Female?" Hoole had never heard these words.

"Yes, you're a male," Berwyck said.

"Are you?"

"Yes, and so is your uncle Grank and so is Theo."

"Have I ever met a female?" Hoole asked.

"I don't think so."

"No," Hoole said firmly. "I *do* think so."

"You have? Where? When?"

"I can't explain it. But I have." Hoole thought of the image in the flames. "I have met her, and I think she might be near."

She, her? How did he even know these terms? Berwyck wondered. And then it just slipped out of Berwyck's beak. He had not meant to say it at all. "I think maybe your mum is dead and you're an orphan."

Hoole's eyes blazed. "Dead like that fish! No, NEVER! She is not dead. I have a mum. Somewhere, someplace. I HAVE A MUM!"

Oh, Great Glaux, what have I started? thought Berwyck. Hoole was almost reeling. He staggered a bit and began to tip over, then pulled himself up tall and straight and, in a

63

quavering voice, now said, "I have a mum and I love her, Berwyck." He blinked. "I mean, I love Uncle Grank. And I love Theo. But I really love my mum. Don't tell them. Please, please, don't tell them that I might love her more."

"Of course, lad, of course. And, Hoole . . ." He paused and fixed him in his amber gaze before continuing. "The world is big enough for all of your love, Hoole. All your love."

Hoole would say nothing of any of this to Grank or Theo. And Berwyck said nothing, either. He had often wondered about Hoole's origins but had never dared to ask. He had, however, assumed that Hoole was of very high birth; one could tell that by his bearing, the way he flew, something in his eyes. But Hoole was profoundly changed from that day on. He became quieter, reflective but not morose. Grank and Theo noticed this but they did not pry. Grank had planned to leave before the end of summer for the Beyond. It would be an ideal time to fly — between the time the katabats finished blowing and before the N'yrthnookah would begin. And Hoole would then be strong enough.

Hoole continued his fishing lessons with Berwyck and even started to acquire a taste for fish. Anchovies were his favorite. But they were very easy to catch as they swam close to the surface and hardly presented a sporting challenge.

One day as they were fishing, Berwyck seemed unusually quiet.

"Anything wrong, Berwyck?"

"No, not really. But I do need to tell you something. Something that might be a little difficult for you to understand."

"Like the male-female thing?"

Berwyck churred. "No, and I think you understood that pretty quickly, lad."

"Sort of," Hoole said. He still had a lot of questions.

"Hoole, I have to go away for a while."

"Where to? Why?"

"It is part of my duty as a Glauxian Brother. We all do this at some time and often more than once. We make what is called a 'pilgrimage.' We become pilgrims."

"Is that like being male or female?"

"Oh, great Glaux in glaumora, no. It is one who takes a journey. When Glauxian Brothers go on a pilgrimage it is to help others."

"Who needs help?"

"I'm not sure right now. But I am certain I shall find someone, some creature."

"Oh." Hoole was confused. "But will you come back? Will I ever see you again?"

"Oh, yes, I'll come back. And yes, if you're still here, I shall see you again."

"I shall miss you terribly, Brother Berwyck. Whom will I fish with?"

"You could teach Theo."

"Yes, but it won't be the same."

"Nothing is ever the same, Hoole. That's what makes life life."

CHAPTER TEN

A Distressed Pygmy

Theo took a pointy stick in his talon and scratched a somewhat lopsided circle in the dirt near his forge. "This is where we are," he said to Hoole. "An island in the middle of this small sea called the Bitter Sea."

"Doesn't the island have a name? If the sea has one, why doesn't the island?"

"I don't know. Interesting question. Would you like to name it?"

"Me?"

Theo wanted to answer: *because you are a prince and will be a king and kings of the N'yrthghar have that privilege.* But he didn't.

"Yes, you."

"I'll try and think of something." Hoole bent closer to the ground. "So what does this sea flow into?"

"The Everwinter Sea," Theo replied.

The lad was naturally curious. An apt pupil, he learned quickly the lessons of geography and of N'yrthghar history. He knew of the great exploits and triumphs of King H'rath, who was killed by Lord Arrin; of H'rath's father, King H'rathmore; of how his forebears had learned to make from ice things that no one had ever dreamed; of how they had not only made weapons for war but things for peace — the ice harps, the first books, called bhags. He knew all about the illustrious line of H'rathian monarchs and yet he had no idea that he was now the last of this line, a prince being made ready to become a king.

For the most part, Theo gave the lessons in geography and the sciences — geology, the art of forging metals, and some celestial navigation. Hoole had by this time learned all the constellations. It was Grank who gave the history lessons and the lessons of government, carefully explaining the knightly codes of honor and service.

"How old do you have to be before you can get to be a knight?" Hoole asked Grank one day.

"Well, it's not simply a question of age. One has to prove oneself. Do something quite extraordinary."

"I am guessing," Hoole said with a small glint in his amber eyes, "that fishing doesn't count. Brother Berwyck said I am an extraordinary fisher owl."

Grank laughed. "No, fishing doesn't count, young'un. But enough lessons for today. Why don't you take yourself off to that cove you so love now that the weather has finally cleared?"

"Phineas? Your name is Phineas?" Hoole asked.

The tiny Pygmy Owl who barely stood as high as Hoole's chest shook his head as if to clear it. This was the first time Hoole had returned to the cove to fish since Berwyck had left. For three days spring storms and tornadoes had raged in the region of the Bitter Sea. When he did come back and perched in an aspen tree — his favorite place for spotting fish — he found it quite incredible that although the ground was littered with the debris of broken branches, the wildflowers still trembled on the forest floor and banks of the cove. Hoole had been contemplating how these tiny fragile things had hung on while entire trees had been stripped of limbs, leaves, and even uprooted when he spotted a tiny dazed owl huddled close to the trunk of the tree on the same branch that he himself was perched.

"Yes, Phineas is my name," the little owl said.

He appeared disheveled and disinclined to talk. Hoole scrutinized him. He had seen so few owls in his short life. Three to be exact. Uncle Grank, a Spotted Owl like himself; Theo, a Great Horned Owl; and Berwyck, a Boreal.

Never had he seen an owl this tiny. Above each eye was a curve of short white feathers that reminded Hoole of minnows. And were those spots of lighter-colored feathers or bars or just smudges?

"What do you call those . . . those things?" Hoole blinked and nodded with his head as if to indicate what he was referring to.

"What things? My wings?"

"I mean those patches of white. Are they spots or bars or what?"

"Or what."

"What?"

"Or what," replied the owl.

Now it was Hoole who was shaking his head in confusion. "What are you talking about?"

"You asked me if my white feathers were spots, bars, or what. They are or whats."

"You mean they are not spots or bars."

"Yes," the owl sighed wearily, "that is what I mean."

Hoole blinked again as if contemplating the "or whats." "They look kind . . . kind of . . ."

"Kind of what?" Phineas asked testily.

"Kind of disorganized."

"You'd be disorganized, too, if you had been tossed about on the edges of tornadoes for three days, sucked up

70

through the Ice Narrows, nearly smacked into a hags-fiend, and then blown here."

"What's a hagsfiend?"

The tiny owl blinked in dismay. "Where have you been all your life?" he asked.

"Here," Hoole replied.

"Look, I'm really tired. I just have to sleep awhile." Phineas closed his eyes tightly, stood rigid, and began to sleep in the classic sleep perch posture of owls outside of hollows.

"Wait — just a couple more questions."

"Oh, Glaux have mercy!" Phineas sighed.

"Are you grown up or what? I mean, you're so weensy."

"Weensy? What a disgusting word." The two little curves of white feathers above Phineas's eyes collided with one another in a frown.

"Small?"

"Slightly better. Yes, I am grown up."

"How up?"

Great Glaux in glaumora, this is the weirdest owl I have ever met. "I hatched a year ago."

"How come you're so small?"

"Because I am a frinkin' Pygmy Owl, and this is how big we grow. What you see is what you get! I mean *really*!"

"All right . . . all right. Calm down," Hoole said.

"Calm down! You calm down! Enough with the questions."

Hoole, of course, ignored that. "Are you male or female?"

Now the Pygmy's beak dropped open. "I am utterly flabbergasted."

"Flabbergasted." Hoole hopped up and down on the branch in delight. "I love that word! I just love that word. Say it again. Please, again."

"FLABBERGASTED! It means shocked beyond ... beyond ..."

At this, Hoole flew straight up in to the air and turned a neat little somersault and landed again.

"Are you from Beyond the Beyond? My uncle Grank talks about Beyond the Beyond all the time."

"Beyond be*lief*!"

"Oh, so that's where you're from — Beyond Belief. I've never heard of that place."

"It's not a place. It is a state of mind! I am a male."

"Me, too! I haven't met a female yet. I was sort of hoping you'd be one. You know, just because I have never met one, but don't worry, you're fine."

"Oh, I am *soo* relieved, because frankly there is very little I can do about it."

"Yeah, I know, I know." Hoole nodded his head quickly and with what he considered great authority. "I know all about that male-female thing. Uncle Grank told me and so did Brother Berwyck." He paused. "Uncle Grank is . . . uh . . . raising me, 'cause I might be an orphan or something but I don't believe it. Anyhow, Brother Berwyck is my friend, a Boreal Owl, but he left a few days ago."

"I think I might have passed him blowing out while I was blowing in."

"Oh, I hope he's all right."

"He looked fine to me. Very strong flier."

"You want to come back to my hollow and meet Uncle Grank and Theo?"

Phineas looked at the young Spotted Owl. It was certainly no use trying to rest here. What did he have to lose? He might get some food and he was too tired to hunt right now himself. "Sure."

"Oh, great!" And Hoole jumped up into the air again and did a somersault finishing with a half twist just before he landed. When he did land, he winked at Phineas. "I'm working on that one. I am aiming for a double twist."

Phineas made a sound, something between a sigh and a groan.

*   *   *

"Uncle Grank, Uncle Grank, Theo! Come out. Come out!" Hoole and Phineas alighted on the branch just outside the hollow. Grank stepped out from the hollow, and Theo flew up from the forge. "This is Phineas. He's a disorganized male Pygmy Owl from Beyond Belief and he's full-grown. And don't call him weensy. But small is all right to say . . . and . . . and oh, I nearly forgot — he said this wonderful new word. He taught it to me: flabbergasted. I just love that word. Say it, Uncle Grank . . . flabber . . . just say it. I know it sounds long — flabber . . ."

"Flabbergasted!" roared Grank. "For Glaux's sake, slow down, Hoole." Grank blinked and shook his head. In so many ways, this little prince was so much like his father, King H'rath. The unbound enthusiasms, the pure joy and delight in owlkind, in life!

"Well, can we keep him?"

"Keep him!" Grank, Theo, and Phineas all hooted in unison.

"Hoole," Grank said sharply. "He is a living thing, an owl. We do not keep living things. We welcome him. Welcome, young Phineas."

"Thank you, sir," Phineas said solemnly, and spun his head toward Hoole. "I am not an object for your passing fancies, I am not an amusement." Hoole wilfed a bit as owls do when they are suddenly intimidated. There was certainly nothing amusing about the little owl right now.

"Yes, yes. Sorry. I understand," Hoole said. "But will you stay for a while? I'll share my vole with you. It was too big to eat all at once. So I just tore off the head for a snack." Hoole hopped up to a notch hole where they stored food and dragged out the headless vole. "It's all yours!"

My Glaux, thought Grank. *If the kingdom is restored and there is ever a court again in the N'yrthghar, how shall I ever prepare this lad for courtly behavior?*

CHAPTER ELEVEN

The Snow Rose Meets Elka

Ygryk and Pleek had landed on the smallest of a cluster of three islands called the Tridents. It was here that Ygryk would perform an ancient charm that would temporarily disguise her for one night and one day as an owl — a Great Horned, the same species as her mate. The run from the Tridents to the Bitter Sea was short, especially with this sudden change of wind, which now came from the south, boosting their speed considerably. Pleek had seen his mate do this transformation just twice before and it always amazed him. The gleaming black feathers grew dull and gradually specks of white began to appear. The dense ruff feathers that grew just under the beak turned white and those on her chest turned gray and became mottled with white patches in a ripplelike pattern. Lastly, the two huge tufts that swept out from every hagsfiend's brow began to shrink and poke up in the manner of a Great Horned's tufts, directly above the eyes, which now had semicircles of white feathers.

While all this was transpiring, Ygryk began to diminish in size; hagsfiends were twice as big as the largest of owls. It took but a short time for this transformation to be completed. And when it was finished, she began talking rapidly to the minute half-hags in the peculiar language of hagsfiends and their parasitic companions. Ygryk was giving them the revised flight plan instructions. With her new body, a new flight formation was necessary for the half-hags. Again Pleek's eyes gleamed with pride. What a creature she was! And if it worked, if indeed they could capture the young son of King H'rath and Queen Siv and change him into a true hagsfiend — not merely an owl with a haggish appearance as he himself had become — if it worked, there would be no limit to their power. Although Lord Arrin had granted them the possibility of keeping this chick for their own, neither Lord Arrin nor any of his top lieutenants knew of the charm that dear Ygryk possessed to transform the owl prince into a hagsfiend. Had they known they would have never permitted the adoption. For Lord Arrin would countenance nothing that might threaten his own power. Secretly, Pleek believed that the reason he had not been permitted into Arrin's inner circle until now was because the lord feared him. He surrounded himself with noddy owls: owls who nodded in constant agreement with him. But now

Lord Arrin needed them because he wanted Siv as his consort as much as Ygryk and Pleek yearned for a chick of their own.

"Ready?" Pleek asked Ygryk.

"Yes." The two birds lifted off the island and set their beaks for the island in the Bitter Sea where the half-hags had tracked Siv.

Siv herself had begun to have odd sensations in her gizzard as she was approaching the Bitter Sea. She was not sure what it was but she felt in some way that she was being followed. The Bitter Sea's westernmost edge lapped the shores of what was called the Nameless, and she decided to fetch up there for a while on a high cliff. The cliffs were notched with deep crevices that were perfect for observing without being observed. She was surprised, however, when she lighted down on the cliff to see an immense Snowy stick her head out from one of these niches. Few birds ever came to the Nameless. It was considered inhospitable and there was a dearth of game. And this was not just any Snowy, but the Snow Rose, the gadfeather she had seen at the gathering at the mouth of the firthkin a few nights before. She was certain she would have noticed a gadfeather passing her in flight, especially this one who wore a strand of red berries woven through her feathers along with silvery tufts of reindeer moss and a dazzling blue plume of a bird she herself had never before seen. The plume was stuck in at a jaunty angle in her head feathers. This was not a bird one could miss.

"Beg your pardon," the Snow Rose asked, "but didn't I see you at the gathering for gadfeathers at the firthkin?"

"Yes, and I heard you sing. Your voice is lovely."

"Oh, thank you. "

"I could never forget it. I have never heard such a voice."

"How kind of you to remember." The Snow Rose blinked. *This Spotted Owl seems different from most gadfeathers,* she thought. She had a kind of elegance that went beyond the moss and various feathers she had tucked into her plumage. Indeed, her gadfeather costume, or gaddis as it was called, was not very special at all. No, there was something else that suggested a deeper elegance, an indefinable grace. "You wouldn't mind, would you . . ." The Snow Rose hesitated for a moment.

"Mind what?" Siv asked.

"If . . . if . . ."

"Yes?"

"If I joined you for a bit on your wanderings?"

Siv truly did not know how to answer. Yes, she would mind, but the Snow Rose was so nice and lovely she hated to appear unfriendly. She had hoped to have some time alone with her son but maybe that was not even a very good idea. She would not be tempted to reveal her identity as his mother with another owl around. She cocked her head and looked at the Snow Rose. "Yes, how nice. I am heading to the island where I understand the Glauxian Brothers have a retreat."

"Do you plan to visit them?"

"Oh . . ." Siv hesitated. "Perhaps. They keep to themselves, you know. Vows of silence and all that. Rather studious, I think."

"Yes, but I once sang for them."

"You did?" Siv was shocked.

"Oh, yes. They enjoy music very much, you know."

"No . . . no, I didn't know," Siv answered.

"And they be quite welcoming to visitors."

Perhaps, Siv thought to herself, *this is not a bad idea at all. If we are with the Glauxian Brothers for a few days it might be easier for me to get away from the Snow Rose to see my son.* But might the Glauxian Brothers remember her from the times they visited in court even disguised as she was?

But I have changed so much, she thought somewhat wistfully. She had been young then, her plumage a rich dark brown with the whitest of spots, not to mention whole wings. No, they would never realize that this dull brown bird with moss and feathers tucked in here and there as if trying to disguise her shabbiness, was in fact Queen Siv, mate of King H'rath.

So at First Black, the two owls rose in the air on a heading for the island in the middle of the Bitter Sea. It was a moonless night and the stars shone brighter because of it as they reached the island. Perhaps if it had not been moonless, Siv would not have spotted the curls of smoke that smudged the deep black of the night. She felt her gizzard quicken. *This must be the place! It has to be one of Grank's fires!* Joy sang through her hollow bones.

"Do you think that's a fire over there?" the Snow Rose asked. "Do you see that smoke?"

"Yes."

"We should go see what's happening."

"Oh, I'd prefer not. I'm tired. You know, this wing gives me trouble and the wind has changed and we're flying against it. I'd like to get to the Glauxian Brothers as soon as we can."

"Oh, yes, I understand . . . er . . ." The Snow Rose

hesitated, then continued. "Don't think me rude. But if we are to be fly mates might you tell me your name?"

Name, name, Siv thought in a panic. *What's my name?* "Elka!" she said suddenly. She remembered that her dear servant, Myrrthe, who had been killed by hagsfiends, had a sister named Elka.

"Elka, a very nice name," the Snow Rose replied.

CHAPTER TWELVE

So Near But Yet So Far

Beneath that curl of smoke in the night sky, Grank perched by the forge, peering into the fire. He simply did not understand. Had he lost his firesight? Oh, he could see images, but they were weak, unclear, and impossible to read. How had this happened? Was it old age? Had his eyesight simply dimmed? His eye tubes shortened up? Had his third eyelids thinned out, letting too much flight debris scar his eyes? It was a mystery and a frustrating one at that for although he could not read the images, the blurry suggestions of contours and shapes set his gizzard trembling. He felt that danger lurked nearby but the images themselves seemed too frail to show him more. It was almost as if the life had been sucked out of them, rendering them hopelessly obscure. When he did see something, it seemed nonsensical. Right now lurking in the bottom part of one very weak flame, he saw what appeared to be a truly immense tree and there were the images of owls hunched over a book of some sort. But what did it all mean?

What Grank had surmised was true. The fire had for him been leeched of its power. For there was another who had firesight. A fire can only yield its images to one fire reader, and it offers them to the reader with the strongest sight. And that was Hoole. For even though his sight was undisciplined, it was amazingly powerful and what was left for Grank were only dim shadowy shapes. Each morning when Grank and Theo slept, Hoole flew down to the forge to watch the image that stirred his gizzard with emotions he had never experienced. He was so obsessed with his vision that he had ignored the other images in the fire.

But had the fire not been drained by Hoole, Grank would have seen much to disturb him. There was no telling if he would have recognized Siv clad in the geegaws of a gadfeather but he certainly would have recognized Pleek and would have surmised that the Horned Owl with whom he flew was none other than Ygryk. Grank knew of the "guise charms," as they were called, of which hagsfiends were capable. And he also knew no other female Great Horned Owl would dare to fly with Pleek since he had taken Ygryk as a mate. He would have also seen Ullryck the assassin following well behind Ygryk with two powerful Great Grays. Indeed, he would have been so agitated that he would have made plans at once to flee this island in the Bitter Sea for Beyond the Beyond. But Grank saw none of this. Yes, he had vague and disturbing feelings in his gizzard but nothing was clear enough to suggest a course of action. He only hoped that his firesight had not left him for good.

"Ah, the Snow Rose!" Brother Fritzel exclaimed. "Our pleasure, madam." A shiver of delight stirred the Snow Rose's white plumage and set the red berries woven through them to jiggling prettily. She had forgotten how polite these brothers were. *Treat me like a queen they do. Might as well be Queen Siv herself.*

"Thank you, brother," she replied.

"You've come at a wonderful time — not a time for silence. So we would love to hear you favor us with a song. And your traveling companion?" Brother Fritzel gave a small bow to Siv.

"Elka," the Snow Rose offered.

"Elka, pleased that you have come here."

Oh, Glaux, thought Siv. *Why couldn't it be a time of silence?* She didn't want to answer questions. But she did know that the brothers were familiar enough with the ways of gadfeathers that they knew better to ask questions about

85

where they had come from or where they were going. So asking her name might be their only question. Still, she was uneasy. She, of course had dozens of questions she wanted to ask them. What did they know of the fire at the end of the island? Had they seen a Spotted Owl, older than herself, near it? Was he accompanied by a young owlet, also a Spotted Owl?

How could her son possibly be so near but yet so far?

Beyond these immediate questions, there was the library that they were in the process of making. The brothers spent countless hours in what they called the cold hollow copying their old inscriptions from ice slabs onto scrolls of birch bark for their books. She would have given anything to poke around in both the cold hollow and the library where they took them once the slabs had been copied. But a gadfeather who could read? A gadfeather even interested in literature? Never. She would betray herself instantly if she showed the least bit of interest in reading.

A second spring storm had begun to lash the Bitter Sea shortly after Siv and the Snow Rose arrived on the island. The retreat of the Glauxian Brothers offered them a safe and cozy refuge. If only Siv could have gone to the library to read, it would have been almost perfect. Then again she was anxious to fly to the other end of the island where she had spotted what she was certain was Grank's fire. Even though she had arrived at a time when vows were relaxed, the brothers were not by any stretch of the imagination a talkative bunch. Still, the first two days she had spent with them had been fruitful. She had picked up a few scant references to three owls at the other end of the island with whom a Brother Berwyck had made contact. A Great Horned Owl, an older Spotted Owl, and a very young Spotted Owl. Her gizzard leaped when she first heard those words "a very young Spotted Owl." But they were known as loners and only Brother Berwyck had been welcomed as a visitor.

"Is Brother Berwyck here now?" Siv tried to sound casual as she asked the question of an elderly Great Gray.

Brother Cedric answered, "He went on his pilgrimage." Most likely, Brother Cedric suggested, through the Ice Narrows to the Southern Kingdoms. At this time, the Southern Kingdoms were hardly kingdoms at all but rather disorganized regions of clanless pioneer owls who, for one reason or another, decided to seek a life in the unknown forests, barren lands, deserts, and prairies to the south. There was no ice there, hardly any snow, unpredictable winds, and a vast and tumultuous sea laced by storms called hurricanes. To go there took courage, but for some to stay on in the Northern Kingdoms with their constant wars and throngs of hagsfiends also took courage. The immense sea of the south never froze and was therefore safe from hagsfiends. But there were no ice weapons, either. Ice was the element on which the lives and culture of the N'yrthghar was based. Life without ice was almost unimaginable. The owls of the N'yrthghar had hundreds of words for ice because there were as many varieties of ice as there were flowers in the Southern Kingdoms. Each type of ice had special qualities. There was issen blaue, blue ice from which special lenses could be ground to protect the eyes even better than the third eyelid when flying through ice storms; there was deep ice, or ice vintygg, for making reflective surfaces; there was a special kind of hard ice that was used for certain weapons; and then the ice from the middle part of the H'rathghar glacier on which the Glauxian Brothers inscribed their books. For most owls of the N'yrthghar, life in the Southern Kingdoms seemed impossible.

So when Brother Cedric said that Berwyck had most likely gone to the Southern Kingdoms for his pilgrimage, Siv replied, "How daring!" As soon as the two words were out she knew she had made a grave mistake. No gadfeather worth her feathers would ever think a flight to the Southern Kingdoms was daring. Gadfeathers knew no boundaries. They went everywhere. They were comfortable in any sky, over any sea. Brother Cedric blinked at her, but asked no further questions. At the same moment, the Snow Rose appeared and said that she was on her way to the upper ring to give a concert.

The retreat of the Glauxian Brothers was a circle of tightly clustered birch trees that stood in the center of a forest that rose on a slight hill in the very middle of the island. The birches were riddled with hollows of all sizes. Some of the hollows were used for study. A very large one had been made into the library. There were hollows for sleeping, small and spare, and then at the very top of the circle of the trees, called the upper ring, the branches of the trees intertwined to form a wonderful platform for various gatherings. It was here that the Snow Rose would give her concert. And so she began.

> *Like a flower at the avalanche's rim*
> *Like a snowflake in the wind*
> *Like a frost picture in the night*
> *Like a star burning, oh, so bright*

Again the song was one of yearning, of longing, of love and loneliness and wandering. There was a sad twang in the Snow Rose's voice and something deep within Siv began to respond, to vibrate. And though there was no ice harp here at the retreat of the Glauxian Brothers, it was as if the slivered icicles of such a harp were within her, trembling in some sort of harmony. *It's like she's singing that song for me!* Siv thought. *She knows my pain, but how could she?*

Siv knew that she could not wait much longer. She had heard some of the brothers muttering under their breaths about hagsfiends in the region. She had tried to dismiss the idea. Why would they dare fly over so much open seawater? But she knew the brothers were wise and did not indulge in idle speculation. She had to act fast. She must fly to the other end of the island. She must see her son. And if there were hagsfiends, she must somehow warn him. Warn him without scaring him to death.

CHAPTER THIRTEEN

"I Know You!"

On the Tridents, the spring gales lashed furiously, and Ygryk glowered as she watched her tawny brown feathers darken and felt the small elegant tufts above her ears grow longer. The charm had worn thin. Waylaid by the headwinds of the gales, they had been blown back to the Tridents three times as they attempted to cross over to the Bitter Sea. And now although the gales had subsided, she knew she must wait at least another three days to try again. Charms — particularly those of transformation — could not be used promiscuously. If so, the transformations were sloppy. She could appear with the ear tufts of a Great Horned Owl and the black shaggy feathers of a hagsfiend. It was also very difficult to use the hypnotic spell of the fyngrot when the spell was weakened.

Meanwhile on the island, Siv watched one of the low-flying storm clouds roll overhead. Hoping not to be seen leaving in the middle of the Snow Rose's concert, she had waited until the cloud bank swept over and then lifted off silently, dissolving into the mist. Within a short time, however, the cloud bank had dispersed, and she found herself flying through a clear and windless night, the new-ing moon no bigger than the finest filament of down.

The words of the song streamed through Siv's mind as she flew out from the upper ring. *A lovely evening for meeting one's son. No, not meeting,* Siv corrected herself. *Seeing. I just want to see him. That's all,* she promised herself. *That's all.*

But, of course, it would not be quite all. There would be more. Siv had planned to fly toward the end of the island where she had spied the smoke rising but as she flew over a cove on the southwest side of the island, she thought she heard the splash of a fishing bird. *A Fish Owl?* she wondered. And being cautious, she thought she should stop and make sure exactly who was about. From hearing the brothers talk, she had thought that there were no other owls except themselves and the three at the very southernmost tip of the island. So Siv alighted in a spruce tree, its branches dense with needles. She watched as she saw not a Spotted Owl nor a Great Horned Owl but a tiny Pygmy attempting to dive for fish in the cove.

"He's just too small. He can't do it, Hoole." The voice was the unmistakable hoot of a Great Horned Owl. Siv saw him fly out from an aspen tree. Then she caught her breath as another young owl flew out. His spots shone like a thousand tiny moons on this nearly moonless night.

"No! No!" the young Spotted Owl protested, as he flew up to the drenched Pygmy who was perched on a log and shaking himself off. "Phineas, you are not too small. No one is too small for anything. You just have to think big!"

Siv caught her breath. She knew this was her son. *And Grank has named him Hoole!* How many times had she heard H'rath before going into battle encouraging his knights in just this way. "Our numbers may be fewer, the hags-fiends may have their charms, their nachtmagen, but we fight for a good cause. We need no charms for we are bold in our gizzards, firm in our task, our wits are keen, and our hearts are strong. They are nothing but flying fakirs and on our side, there is discipline. Nachtmagen is cheap, and we are owls of quality, of passion, of commitment." This, indeed, was the son of H'rath! She watched him for hours, until the night melted into the dawn.

Night after night, she returned but always Hoole was in the company of the owl named Phineas or the Great Horned Owl he called Theo. Once he came with Grank and she saw that Grank had aged. Her gizzard trembled at the sight of him. He seemed smaller than she had remembered. Could he take care of Hoole until the owlet was safely grown up? *But what must I look like?* she thought. *I, too, have aged and with this mangled wing I must appear piteous.* Although she longed for the other owls to go away so she could approach Hoole, she was at the same time happy they were there. They must be a help to Grank.

Then one night when she came, she saw that Hoole was alone and diving with abandon into the cove. *Would it be so wrong if I just flew down there and talked to him?* she thought. *I'm a gadfeather, after all. Gadfeathers go everywhere and talk to everyone. Nothing unusual about that.*

Siv lighted down on the end of the branch where Hoole perched. He blinked at the strange Spotted Owl. It wasn't the oddly shaped wing that startled him. It was all the stuff she had tucked into her plumage — feathers from other birds, bits of moss, and even a few berries.

"What are you?" he asked her. "And why are you wearing all that . . . that stuff?"

"I'm a gadfeather," Siv answered. She hadn't thought that because of the extreme isolation of this island, Hoole might never have seen a gadfeather before. "You haven't heard of gadfeathers?"

"No, and my uncle Grank teaches me a lot."

Siv felt a pulse quicken in her gizzard. *He calls Grank uncle.*

At the very same time Hoole felt a deep stirring in his

own gizzard. He took a step closer to her. Siv began to quiver all over. This was her son! H'rath's son. She desperately fought the urge to preen him, to run her beak through his feathers, to pick out mites, debris. She must not. Hoole was looking at her hard. It was almost as if he were peering right into her gizzard, which was in a complete tumult.

"I know you," he said suddenly.

Siv began to wilf, so great was her alarm. She shook her head. "Oh, no, my dear, I am sure you don't."

"But I do. I . . . I . . . I saw you in the fires, the flames."

Great Glaux, thought Siv. *He can read flames. He's a fire reader! Like Grank! Does Grank know?*

"I saw you coming," he continued. "I wanted you to come."

"You did?"

"Yes, yes. I can't explain this but there's been . . ." He hesitated. ". . . like a hole, yes, a hole in my gizzard. I didn't really know it was there until I saw you in the flames. But now that you are here the hole is filled." He blinked in utter amazement at this sudden realization. "You have to come back to the hollow with me. You have to meet Uncle Grank and Theo and Phineas. Phineas is my best friend. Well, so is Theo but, you know, he's older and

Phineas is closer to my age." Hoole was speaking rapidly now. "Please, please, come right away. Stay with us. Stay with us forever!"

"But I can't, dear," Siv replied.

"Why not?" He was stunned.

"I just can't."

"Give me one good reason."

"It's just . . . it's just . . ."

"Just what?" Hoole demanded.

"I have family. I have chicks to attend."

"No!" Hoole almost wailed. "You can't have any-one else!"

"But I do!" It broke Siv's heart and shattered her gizzard to lie like this.

Hoole began to wilf right in front of her eyes. Siv felt desperate. What could she do to help this poor young owl, her very own son? Was this not the cruelest thing that had ever happened to her? To have to deny one's own son! And just at that moment two owls melted out of the night. Two Great Horned Owls, or so Siv thought. It sud-denly felt as if a bolt of lightning had coursed through Siv's gizzard. One of the owls, despite its tawny feathers and two ear tufts, had a . . . a haggish look.

It's Ygryk!!! Siv's brain reeled at the recognition. "Fly, Hoole, fly!" she screamed.

CHAPTER FOURTEEN
"Mother!"

"A stranger, you say, Phineas?" Grank asked. "What did he look like."

"It wasn't a he. It was a she. A gadfeather, and beneath all those things they always wear, I think she was a Spotted Owl."

"A Spotted Owl!" Grank said and lofted himself off his perch in alarm.

Phineas was now alarmed himself. "You told me that if I ever saw a strange owl in these parts I should come and tell you immediately."

"You did right, young'un. You did right!"

Then at that very moment they heard a shrill cry coming from the cove.

"Theo! Come quick," Grank called. "You stay here, Phineas. It's too dangerous for a small owl like you."

Hoole didn't know what was happening. A large owl was flying directly toward him and the other, a Great

Horned — but not Theo — was flying toward the gad-feather.

"What's happening?" he cried out. He did not see that still another Great Horned was flying toward him.

"Fly!" the gadfeather screamed again.

But it was too late. Strange little flying creatures had darted out from under the wings of the Great Horned who was attacking him.

"Meebla yeben yip," said the Great Horned Owl.

What was this strange language she was speaking? And nowthatthesawherupcloseshedidn'treallylooklikeaGreat Horned. Her feathers were raggedy and almost black. One of the small creatures attending her flew up to him and pricked him in the wing. Instantly, he felt his wings lose their power. *I am going yeep*, Hoole thought. *Uncle Grank told me about going yeep, but I never thought it would happen to me.* He crumpled to the ground on his back. Opening his eyes wide, he saw the Great Horned bending over him. A strange yellow light was pouring like a liquid river of gold from her eyes. Then her dark beak was coming closer and closer. "Open wide, my darling, open wide." Her talon was coming straight for his eye.

Hoole saw the Spotted Owl flying straight down, her talons set to rake the back of the Great Horned who was leaning over him. Suddenly, another Great Horned, the mate of this one, appeared from behind the Spotted. He heard a sound like the clank of Theo's hammer and above him there was chaos. Complete chaos.

"MOTHER!" Hoole screamed and that was the last he remembered. The world went blank, not dark, but blank.

The brothers had suspected right from the start that the Spotted Owl who called herself Elka was not who she said she was. She wasn't a gadfeather. Of this the Snow Rose was also fairly sure. When Elka had replied with that peculiar remark to Brother Fritzel about the pilgrim brother being so daring, she was absolutely certain. Nonetheless, the Snow Rose had grown fond of the Spotted Owl and admired how she had flown so boldly and without complaint despite her maimed port wing. Gadfeathers, however, never pried. It was not in their nature. At least the Snow Rose thought so until she found herself flying toward the southern tip of the island. *Why am I doing this?* she thought. *Why? Gadfeathers are not supposed to have any attachments.* But she had seen Elka fly off into that rolling cloud bank during her concert. Ever since that night she noticed that Elka would often slip away, giving no explanation. Not only that, Elka had grown progressively quieter and withdrawn into her own thoughts. So, determined to find out what was drawing her away, on this night the Snow Rose decided to follow her.

She stayed a good distance behind so she would not be detected and when she came to the cove she found a leftover bank of snow that provided her with the perfect camouflage. Standing straight and very still, she stretched upward and compressed her plumage, blending perfectly into the snowbank. With one eye opened a fraction of a slit, she had been observing the strange interactions between Elka and the young Spotted Owl.

What is going on here? she thought as she saw the young Spotted Owl grow more anxious, demanding that Elka come with him. Then suddenly two large Great Horned Owls appeared on the opposite side of the cove. That was when Elka shreed, "Ygryk!" and the tranquillity of the cove had been shattered. The two stranger owls swooped down on Elka and the young one.

At the precise moment that Hoole screamed "MOTHER!" a white mass of feathers laced through with bits of twigs and berries — the Snow Rose — shot across the cove like a hurling ice devil blown off a ridge of the H'rathghar glacier. White feathers spun up in the night as she collided with Pleek. Then there was a swirl of feathers — tawny ones of a Great Horned, the rich brown of a Spotted Owl, and the gleaming black of a hagsfiend!

Four owls tumbled through the air in a knot of fury as Pleek, the Snow Rose, Siv, and Ygryk fought high above the cove.

The Snow Rose blinked and staggered briefly in flight. *Great Glaux!* A hagsfiend had appeared exactly where a Great Horned had been an instant before.

And Pleek was now plunging down from above the cove in a death spiral with his talons extended toward the Snow Rose. Suddenly, there was a bright gleam in the night, and Pleek was knocked out of the spiral. The Snow Rose peeled off in flight. She flipped her head back to see what was happening and gasped as she saw blood coursing down the Great Horned's face into his eyes. Above him was another owl who had the strangest talons. But they were not talons. They were more like claws and appeared much sharper, shining brightly in the night. As bright as the fyngrot the hagsfiend was now desperately trying to cast upon Theo, armed with battle claws.

The Snow Rose looked around for Elka. Where was she?

Phineas flew down to Hoole and tried to drag him to safety as above him four owls clashed in the night.

The older Spotted Owl, Grank, suddenly flew in the face of the hagsfiend and, shouting in the strange language of half-hags, said, "H'blen b'shrieek micht garmish schmoot."

The hagsfiend's wings began to fold and from underneath them the tiny half-hags fell into the cove's water. The hagsfiend herself looked down in horror.

Then the Snow Rose witnessed something she had never in all her life seen before. The wounded Great Horned, Pleek, dived toward the water. Just as the hagsfiend's wing dipped into the cove, he pulled her free. The Great Horned Owl with the strange talons tore off after them.

"Let them go, Theo," Grank called. "Let them go. They won't get far. Help me over here." Then he turned his attention to Hoole. "Let me see your eyes, Hoole. Can you open your eyes? Can you see?" Grank's voice trembled with terror.

Of course, I can open my eyes, Hoole thought. *Why is he going on about my eyes?* Hoole blinked. He had never in his short life seen Grank look so terrible. His beak quivered, his eyes were filled with a dark amber terror. "What's wrong with you?"

Grank uttered a strange noise halfway between a sob and a gulp from deep inside his throat. "Glaux bless, she didn't get one," Grank said with relief drenching his voice.

"One what?" Hoole asked.

"Your eye. An old hagsfiend charm. It must have been Ygryk who attacked you."

Hoole was now fully alert. "Where did she go?"

"Don't worry," Grank said. "The hagsfiend will never last. Pleek can't support her that long in flight. He'll drop her into the sea."

"I don't know what a hagsfiend is. I want to know where my mother went."

"Your mother?" Grank was stunned.

"I told you I saw a Spotted Owl," Phineas said, lighting down next to Grank.

"What are you doing here? I thought I told you to stay back. You aren't big enough."

"I'm big enough to have seen that Spotted Owl Hoole is talking about and how she attacked the Great Horned. Right before Theo came in and then a Snowy hurled out of nowhere."

"She was here?" Grank spoke in a dazed voice. His gizzard was in a complete twirl.

"Her name is Elka." The Snow Rose flew down from the spruce she had been perched in.

"I don't care what her name is. She's my mother and I want her."

"Oh, Great Glaux!" Grank tipped his head up and shook it.

There wasn't a breeze. The surface of the cove's water was like a mirror and floating on top — scattered like dead insects — were the bodies of half-hags. Their poison had already begun to contaminate the cove. Fish were floating to the top, gasping for air. But the five owls paid no heed.

The Snow Rose wondered why Elka has vanished so suddenly.

Theo stared forlornly at the blood on his battle claws, his gizzard in deep anguish. *But had there been a real choice?* he wondered.

Hoole kept blinking his eyes. *Why would anyone want to blind me?*

Grank had composed himself. He would say nothing of the true identity of the owl who called herself Elka. His only thoughts were about leaving. They had to leave and leave fast. He turned to Theo, Phineas, and Hoole. "We must all of us fly — fly away from here. Others might be coming. The war is too close now." Then turning to the Snow Rose he said, "You are welcome to join us, friend." The Snow Rose dipped her head, abashed and delighted. No owl who was not a gadfeather had ever called her "friend" before. Not even Elka. But she shook her head. "No, I still have some wandering to do. But thank you, thank you ever so much."

"Think nothing of it," Grank replied.

But she would think much of it. She would remember

that someone who was not a gadfeather had called her "friend."

"But I want my mother to come back," Hoole said.

"If she found you here, she will find you again, Hoole. But it is far too dangerous for us to remain here. We must go now. We cannot delay another second."

"But where are we going?" Hoole asked

"To Beyond the Beyond," Grank replied. He swiveled his head to the south and blinked as if he could see that distant fiery land.

"To the Beyond!" Theo gasped, hardly disguising his excitement. Grank had told him so much about the Beyond and their fires. Finally, he would be going to that land where Grank had learned to dive into the fires of the volcano and retrieve coals. Grank referred to himself as a collier, or carrier of coals. He was the only owl who could do this. He had promised someday to teach Theo. But he often would say that colliering was a waste of time for Theo, who was so gifted in the art of blacksmithing. "I would hate to see you squander your talents, lad. If I am the first collier in the world of owls, you are certainly the first blacksmith. I shall bring you all the coals you'll ever need and you shall make tools you have yet to dream of. Not just weapons, Theo."

At last, thought Theo, they would be going to that

land of coals. Coals and embers of infinite variety with which they could build fires of all kinds of intensities in which he could smith metal into all sorts of tools. Theo knew that time was of the essence now. Had it really been Queen Siv who had attacked the Great Horned? Had she told Hoole that she was his mother? All these questions raced through Theo's mind.

His thoughts were interrupted now by Phineas, who was telling Grank that he, too, must go to the Beyond.

"Don't tell me I'm too small to go that far. I can fly as well as any of you."

"I want him to come," Hoole said firmly. "If I can't have my mother, I want my best friend."

Phineas's eyes sparkled as Hoole said this. "Am I really your best friend, Hoole?"

"Yes," Hoole said and then suddenly swiveled his head toward Theo. "Theo, you're not just a friend, you're like my big brother. No, not like. You are." Hoole paused. "And, Grank, if you were not here, I would miss you as much as I am now missing my mother. You are both mother and father to me." *Brother Berwyck was right,* he thought. *I do have enough love for everyone.*

"But how do you know, young'un, that this Spotted Owl is really your mother?" Grank had expected Hoole to say something like "I just know it" or "I feel it in my gizzard." But he said neither. "I saw it in the fire, Uncle Grank." Grank was stunned. He leaned in closer to Hoole. "You saw it in the fire?"

Hoole nodded.

"What did you see in the fire? When?"

"I should have told you, but one day when I was flying over the fire in the forge, something caught my eye in the flames — a shape. And there was something in that shape that made me feel wonderful. It drew me to it. But I didn't want to go see it any closer until I could do it alone. Theo was working with his tongs. So I sneaked out when you were both sleeping." He blinked at Grank. It was the kind of blink young owls often gave when they were slightly ashamed, when they were caught being disobedient.

"Go on, lad," Grank said in a gentle tone.

"Well, I just knew that this shape, this thing was coming for me. It made me feel all warm inside. I felt this terrible longing. I knew that I would never be whole until she came. Even though I wasn't sure what it was, what the shape was, I knew it was a she, that I belonged to her and she belonged to me. I would be made complete when she came. So every dawn I snuck down and watched the flames."

"I see now," Grank began to speak slowly. "I see now why it happened."

"Why what happened? Are you angry, Uncle Grank?"

"No, lad. It's just that you are a fire reader — like me. Only your vision is stronger, much stronger, and that is why there were no images left for me to read in the flames."

"I'm sorry, Uncle Grank. I'm really sorry. I didn't mean to."

"Don't be sorry, lad. You have a gift. You can read deep into the flames."

"Fire reader?" Phineas said.

"Never heard of such a thing." The Snow Rose looked at Theo as if for an explanation.

But Theo could say nothing. He was just looking at Hoole and remembering the peculiar luminosity of the egg from which this owl had hatched. This owl, this prince was special. If there was any creature on earth who could save the N'yrthghar and quell the hagsfiends and their poisonous magic, it must be Hoole. But for now he must not know that he is a prince and a future king. No one must know. They must fly immediately to the Beyond. *Yes,* thought Theo, *and like the metals I work with in my fires, young Hoole will be tempered and wrought into a king.*

Into a king!

CHAPTER FIFTEEN
A Wolf Howls

The wolf called Fengo sat on a high ridge and, with his head thrown back, he began to howl. His strange mad music, wild and untamed, threaded through the night that glowed with the fires of the volcanoes. There are many ways in which a wolf howls, most of them understandable to other wolves. Through their howling and scent marking they speak of danger, of the territorial boundaries, of herds of caribou to be hunted. But sometimes they simply howl — not to communicate, but to mourn or wail messages meant only for themselves or for Lupus. It was to the constellation they called Lupus, that great wolf of the sky, that Fengo now howled.

Where is he? Where is he? Where is Grank?
Never gone so long.
Has he been killed?
Does he now climb the spirit trail,
Lupus?

The good owl, friend of mine.
He is owl. I am wolf.
He is sky. I am earth.
We are brothers of this world.

This particular kind of howling was called glaffing, and it was considered poor form to interrupt a glaffing wolf. But another wolf began to climb the ridge where Fengo howled. Fengo did not stop but rose to his feet, the hackles on the back of his neck stiffened, his ears raised now, and his tail lifted in a line horizontal with his spine. The approaching wolf, MacHeath, began to crouch and pull back his mouth into a grimace. With his belly scraping the ground and his ears laid back flat, he started to move forward toward Fengo in an attitude of complete submission.

How dare he approach me when I am glaffing. Such swine, these MacHeaths! Fengo continued glaffing, trying to ignore the wolf. But his mind was drawn to other thoughts. *Why did I even bother to include the MacHeaths on our journey from the Always Cold.* The wolves led by Fengo had left the land far to the west that had once been hospitable but had grown colder and colder, colder even than the N'yrthghar, until every river and stream and pond was frozen and even the waterfalls were stilled. They had made the long journey that had taken countless moons to this land of Beyond the Beyond where fires scorched the sky and the land never froze. Fengo paid no heed to the wolf and continued his glaffing for Grank. Never had Grank been gone so long, and deep in his bones Fengo felt that something awful must have happened to his dear friend since a messenger came and delivered the letter from King H'rath so many moon cycles ago. When Fengo finished, he turned to MacHeath. He loathed this wolf who was full of senseless rage, a hunger for power and who, in his fury, had been known to kill both mates and pups.

"Yes? What is it?" Fengo growled.

"I would like to serve, Fengo."

Fengo knew what was coming. MacHeath had seen Grank retrieve the owl ember from one of the volcanoes. Many wolves had seen it, and they sensed its peculiar power. They were smart enough to stay away from it. But not MacHeath. He had been fascinated by the ember and the strange owl who had stared into its depths. He waited now for a reply from Fengo. Fengo remained silent. This exasperated the impulsive MacHeath. "He was right, you know," he said with an edge in his voice.

"Who was right about what?" Fengo replied.

"The owl, the one called Grank, the one you are glaffing for. He was right when he called it the wolf ember.

It is not the owl ember. It holds the same green fire that burns in our eyes." He dropped his lids halfway so that only a slit of fierce green showed.

"The ember is not all green. There is the fiery orange of its heat and the blue . . ."

MacHeath interrupted, "But the blue of the center is ringed with green — green like our eyes, Fengo!"

Fengo was now incensed. His hackles grew more erect. He snarled, humped up his back, and advanced on MacHeath. But MacHeath did not move. He pulled back his lips, baring his teeth in the grin of submission, and made an odd sound halfway between a growl and a whine. He was caught between fear and aggression, threat and submission. His hackles were erect yet his ears were laid back. And still he crouched and made the whinish growls. Would it be submission or aggression? It was the utter contempt in Fengo's eyes that triggered him. He suddenly exploded in a high leap and came down on Fengo, his fangs sinking into Fengo's shoulder. MacHeath was huge, larger than Fengo, massively built. But Fengo was a cunning fighter. He immediately sank down close to the ground. His goal was to reach the slope and let gravity do the work for him. He flipped himself once, twice, and then a third time and rolled. Together, they rolled off the ridge and down the slope. MacHeath held on. Fengo suddenly twisted his neck around, and although he intended to grab MacHeath's snout with his teeth, he missed and his fangs sank into one eye. There was a terrible howl of pain and MacHeath finally let go.

But Fengo was not done with this wolf yet. He would not kill him, but he had to prove that he, Fengo, was dominant. He must show the other wolves who was leader. So, as MacHeath attempted to run away, Fengo dragged him back. Blood poured from MacHeath's eye socket and on the ground lay the eyeball.

"There is your ember, wolf. The bloody eyeball of greed! The bloody eyeball of your tyranny. Your mates will suffer your abuse no more. Your pups will no longer cower." Fengo then turned to the other wolves who had gathered at the foot of the slope. "Often I have told you that it was not I who led you here, but the spirit of a long-dead hoole. Hoole, the wolf word for owl and the name of the very first owl. So we say that this ember is not the wolf ember but the owl ember. And it is our duty to guard it until the owl who will be king comes."

"Fengo." It was Dunmore MacDuncan, a young but very intelligent wolf who was just a pup when they had left the Always Cold and begun their journey to the Beyond. Dunmore had impressed Fengo from the start, for not only was he wise beyond his years but, despite a birth injury that had left him with a deformed leg, he was brave and stalwart and never gave up. He ran as hard and as long as the other wolves on the long journey, and never complained. Not only that, Dunmore seemed to possess a rare intuition. He sensed danger before anyone else. His instincts were finely honed. He was quick of mind and body despite his leg. Now Dunmore crouched down submissively and made the sign for asking a question.

"Yes, Duncan."

"Will this owl be our king as well?"

"He will not be our king but he will help us. We know little of magic and what the owls of the N'yrthghar call nachtmagen. But there are practitioners of this terrible kind of magic in the north who are known as hagsfiends. They want to rule not only over the owls, but all creatures. They cannot easily cross open seas and if they touch salt water it can wound them mortally. They hope with their magic to be able to find a charm that will guard them against seawater, and if they do that, we shall all be in danger."

"And what if the wrong owl comes for the ember?" Dunmore MacDuncan asked.

How smart this young wolf is, Fengo thought. Indeed, Fengo himself had been absorbed for a long time with this same question. So far, Grank was the only owl who knew how to dive for coals, but owls were smart and in the kingdom of owls, news traveled. Fengo felt that it would not be long before other owls might master the art of colliering and the craft of making tools from metals. How, indeed, would they prevent some tyrannical owl, like one of those who had betrayed King H'rath, from hearing about the ember and making an attempt to retrieve it? There were five volcanoes that stood in a circle. When Grank had finally given up the ember, he had dropped it into the one they called Stormfast. But there was no certainty that it would remain there. Underlying the volcanoes was a network of rivers flowing with lava. The ember could move to any of the other volcanoes. He wondered if he should set up a watch to guard the ember. He would mull this over in his mind. Perhaps Dunmore MacDuncan would be the perfect wolf to captain such a watch over this ring of volcanoes.

He looked on now with great interest as the wolves dispersed. Which of MacHeath's mates would stay with him. And which would leave? He saw MacHeath approaching each one, undoubtedly with new promises and favors. Indeed, they all stayed with him — all except one! Hordweard. She was the oldest of his mates. Perhaps at long last she was tired of his abuse. For ears she had only stubs. MacHeath had bitten them off in a fit of rage when she had not laid them back in submission quickly enough. Or perhaps she was beyond bearing any more cubs ... *Or perhaps,* thought Fengo, *she is a traitorous old she wolf. Had he convinced her to spy for him? After all, MacHeath is missing one eye now. Why not have three! What has he promised Hordweard?* MacHeath held a power over his mates that was hard to escape despite his abusive treatment. He controlled them not only with physical force but with threats and bribes. Fengo sincerely doubted that a wolf as old and weakened Hordweard would dare leave him for long.

CHAPTER SIXTEEN

The Hagsfiend of the Ice Narrows

A bizarre-looking bird with a fat orange beak, beady black eyes, and shaggy feathers cautiously waddled up to Pleek and offered him some small fish that it had just dived for. Pleek shook his head once more in disbelief as he watched this peculiar concoction of a bird. Half-hagsfiend, half-puffin, and strangest of all, it could dive with immunity into the sea and fish like all puffins. The salt water did not harm him.

For the cycle of one moon, Pleek and Ygryk had been sheltered in the Ice Narrows by Kreeth, the old hagsfiend who was Ygryk's friend. Both he and Ygryk were recovering from their wounds. But Pleek wondered if his dignity would ever fully recover. How could Lord Arrin have turned on them so? Halfway back to the Ice Narrows they had been set upon by Lord Arrin's most cunning assassin: Ullryck.

If Kreeth had not been flying by with two of her monstrosities they would never have survived the flight over the Bitter Sea. But she was a powerful hag and what she lacked in strength and size, she more than made up for in the power of her charms. "Kreeth, why would Lord Arrin send Ullryck to kill us? If it hadn't been for you and your two . . . puff-hags, we would never have made it back here."

Kreeth thought hard for a long moment as she gazed about her cave. It was like a laboratory of nachtmagen. Gizzards of owls and other birds she had murdered were neatly dried and hung up. There were salt stars that had formed in the evaporated lakes of the Nameless and several petrified bird eggs that she had excavated from a region she would not reveal. The entire ice cave was strung with macabre garlands of withered eyeballs. Finally, she turned to Pleek and spoke: "Most obviously, Ullryck was spying on you and Ygryk. When she saw Ygryk trying to . . . remove the young owl's eye, she must have thought she was trying to kill him. So she planned her own attack."

Pleek nodded. Kreeth pointed to one of the withered eyeballs that hung above her. "Got that one from a polar bear. Imagine that," she cackled. "Me going after a polar bear. But I got him, and I started pouring the fyngrot into him. But he got away. Still, cursed be the creature that encounters a polar bear with fyngrot."

"Does he know how to use it?" Pleek asked.

"Can't tell you. And if he does know how, will he have the gallgrot to use it? You see, this is what is so interesting about my work. It is both nachtmagen, and scientific and philosophical." She paused. "And it takes a unique courage. What other hagsfiend would live so close to open water? It is what my dear mum told me: Keep your friends close and your enemies closer. The sea is my enemy, but I have spent a lifetime here in the Ice Narrows studying it. I shall one day divine a charm that will render salt water powerless against us."

"Pleek, Kreeth, come quickly!" Ygryk spun her head around from where she had been looking out of the cave. "Look there in the distance, coming through the Narrows...."

"By Glaux," whispered Pleek. In the fog of the Ice Narrows, the forms of four owls could be seen: Grank, Hoole, Phineas, and Theo.

"Are those the claws you were telling me about?"

"Yes," Pleek's voice quavered and the wound that ran down his back where new feathers were just beginning to fledge twinged painfully. Never would he forget the tearing of those claws on his back.

"Hmmm, I don't think it's wise to attack," Kreeth said thoughtfully. "They are four, all armed except for the Pygmy, and neither of you is ready to fight."

Ygryk looked down at the roiling water that churned through the Ice Narrows. A wave of nausea overcame her. She had to step back from the edge of the cave. She was a long way from fighting. Most of her half-hags had died in the cove. It would be many moon cycles before the remaining ones could reproduce enough for battle. Therefore her poison levels were down. It would be a long time. And would she ever dare fly over open water again?

But Pleek's eyes were bright. "They must be heading for Beyond the Beyond. That would be the most sensible place to hide out, across a vast sea and then to the farthest reaches of a broad continent. What Lord Arrin wouldn't give for this information! Ha! But, Ygyrk, we have it. Don't you see?"

"See what, dear Pleek?"

"We can still have our son and that son means power."

"Indeed, it does!" Kreeth said in a low voice. "With that young prince, I think I could complete the charm that would shield us all from open water. We could bring nachtmagen to the Southern Kingdoms." She turned to Pleek and Ygryk. "We could rule!"

CHAPTER SEVENTEEN

A Seedling

"Are we halfway there yet, Uncle Grank?" Hoole asked as they left the Ice Narrows.

"Not yet, Hoole. I told you it is a long journey. We have to fly all the way across the sea of the Southern Kingdoms."

"Is it green like our seas?"

"Believe it or not, I have yet to see the color of its water. The Southern Sea is always thick with fog. Once the fog thinned toward the middle and I saw that below me was an island."

"Were there any trees to perch in for a rest?" Theo asked.

"Not a one. Bare as can be. Not a living thing. Just rocks. But we can still go down and take a rest if I can find the island again."

It was shortly after that the fog started to clear and patches of blue sky began to break through. "My, we are lucky!" Grank said. And then all at once every scrap of fog, every cloud seemed to evaporate and the sun was shining warmly.

"Look! There's the island!" Hoole shouted.

The four owls began their descent, circling in steeply banking turns that grew tighter and tighter.

From the very first moment that Hoole saw the island he felt as if his gizzard were singing. By the time they landed, he was in a state. He hadn't felt such stirrings since he had first glimpsed his mother's figure in the flames of the forge's fire. Reminded of his mother, he once again felt that painful wrench in his gizzard and his heart. He drooped his head. A tear fell to his feet. The three other owls noticed that Hoole was experiencing something more than just a rest in a long flight. He seemed to be in some sort of trance.

"A gizzard dream," Grank whispered to himself.

Hoole continued to look down. He peered harder as he spied infinitesimally small movements in the dirt. The kind of movements one might find in the N'yrthghar in a pile of snow when the ice worms stirred in late winter or in the Southern Kingdoms when an anthill is disturbed and the grains of dirt begin their minute writhing as the ants flee. But this movement was not that of ice worms or ants. It was a seedling pushing from the ground.

"Uncle Grank."

"Yes, lad?"

"You're wrong."

"Wrong about what, Hoole?"

"This island is not bare. There are living things here."

"What?" Grank, Theo, and Phineas all asked at once.

"A tree is starting to grow. Right here."

The others came to where Hoole was standing and peered down. Between his feet a small green sprout pushed up from the earth. As soon as it was clear of the dirt, its top sprung up.

"By Glaux! I believe it's a seedling tree," Grank murmured.

"Look, it's growing so fast!" Phineas said. "It's almost as tall as I am."

"I've never seen anything like it." Grank gasped. "I don't know how it's possible for a tree to grow so quickly. Oh, dear. I hope it's not some nachtmagen."

The
seedling seemed to tremble at the sound of the word.

"Oh, no!" Hoole said. "Never nachtmagen. This is a good tree . . . It has . . . Ga', Uncle Grank. Yes, Ga'."

"But only owls have Ga'," Theo said.

"No. Not just owls. This tree has Ga'," Hoole said firmly.

By the time they left, the tree was almost as tall as Hoole. Oddly enough, as soon as they flew out to sea the fog closed in thickly, leaving no trace of island or tree. When they were far way from the island and approaching Cape Glaux, which jutted out into the Southern Sea, unbeknownst to them the tree was larger than either Grank or Theo.

From Cape Glaux they set course almost due north for the Beyond, even though this was not the most favorable direction in terms of the wind. But Grank wanted to avoid the more populated areas in the Shadow Forest and Silverveil and in particular any grog trees where owls gathered to drink the potent berry juice and to exchange gossip and news. The fewer owls they saw, the better.

Hoole was disappointed. He had wanted very much to see the beautiful green forests of Silverveil that he had heard about from Berwyck, and he had even hoped to meet up once again with the Glauxian Brother.

They fetched up for the night on the very edge of the Shadow Forest that pressed hard against a spirit woods. This was not an ideal place, either, for spirit woods were said to be haunted by the scrooms of dead owls who had not quite finished their business on earth. Grank would have to keep a close eye on the young'un.

That morning they settled into a hollow in a fir tree. It had definitely seen one too many storms and as it creaked violently in the least wind, Grank had an uneasy feeling in his gizzard.

"Now, you stay put, lad. No getting up, no sneaking out for a little morning flight. You need your rest. Remember, when we get to the Beyond, you'll need all your energy."

"Yes, Uncle Grank. You're going to teach me to collier, aren't you?"

"I promised, didn't I?"

"That you did."

But it was more than colliering that Grank wanted to teach Hoole in the Beyond. He needed to teach the young'un about the wolves. He would need Fengo's help for that. And Fengo must also teach Hoole how to listen to the various sounds of the volcanoes. Each one of the five volcanoes produced a variety of different sounds. It was not unlike the ice harps that the gadfeathers played, that were said to have their moods depending on the time of day, the weather, the time of the year. So, too, the volcanoes seemed to have their moods. Grank himself had been hopeless in interpreting them. He now looked back on that day that he had retrieved the ember as one of pure accident. Yes, the side of the volcano had seemed to turn transparent and suddenly it was as if he could see into the very heart, the gizzard, of this one volcano. He spied the ember as it had bubbled to the surface. Quickly, he made a dive for it and as soon as he grasped the ember he had felt its power.

But for Grank, it had been too powerful, and a strange interlude ensued in which he grew lethargic and uncaring. For all of the ember's power, Grank had failed to exploit or use any of it. He was simply overcome, and finally Fengo told him plainly that he was not equal to the power of the ember and urged him to put the ember back. Later, the wolf had said that he was eternally grateful that the ember was retrieved by a good owl like Grank and not an evil owl, a graymalkin, who would not slip into lethargy as Grank had but sink to profound evil.

But, Grank thought, was Hoole that owl of both goodness and power? Was his power such that he would be neither vanquished by it nor use it for tyranny or nachtmagen? And even if Hoole were such a good owl, as Grank suspected, it was not a given that he would know how to use the power wisely and with compassion. For this, an owl must be prepared, raised in the way of Ga'. So far, he had tried his best, but was it good enough?

Grank thought about all this as he tried to sleep in the growing light of the morning. Failure to do his proper duty by Hoole was unacceptable, unthinkable. Forget courtly behavior with all its affectations. How could he have ever worried about such trivialities with Hoole? He must raise a prince to be a king. A king must be tempered like metal. He thought of how Theo worked with the metals in the forge for the battle claws. He heated the metal until it was white-hot and then hammered it, then folded it and hammered it again. Through this constant cycle of heating and hammering and folding, he made claws that were strong yet flexible. That was how a prince must be tempered to be a king. Strong enough for any battlefield, any war, but tempered with compassion and wisdom so that he knows the richness of restraint, the fruitfulness of peace, and the grace of mercy. And just such a king was now desperately needed.

By noon, as streaks of sun washed into the hollow where they slept, Grank gave up on sleep and wandered out in search of a vole, or perhaps a weasel.

He had flown over one of the few meadows in the region and looked for the tracks of a ground animal in the tall grass. He found one and began to follow it and did not notice that it led right into the pale trees of the spirit woods before it dwindled to nothing. He sighed deeply for now he was truly hungry, having anticipated a plump rat or rabbit or vole at the end of the track. He jerked his head quickly as he heard a sigh as if in answer to his own. It couldn't be an echo. There was nothing in this place to create an echo. He had alighted on a bare mound where the path had ended. Surely a weasel or mole or whatever rodent he had been chasing did not sigh. But he heard it again. A sound not so much like a sigh but a ragged expiration of breath. He stood perfectly still, his feathers becoming flatter and flatter against his body. He saw something in the tree ahead of him, gathering like mist.

It was H'rath — the scroom of H'rath. He was thankful that at least it was he in these woods and not Hoole. He had never encountered a scroom before, but his grandmother had, and she had told him that one must wait for the scroom to speak. She'd told him it was not like speaking at all but that the words seemed to fill your head. It was a very peculiar way of hearing and communicating. And it was incomplete. The scrooms could rarely tell you everything, though they seemed to know what was going on in your own mind. So much so that when one was communing with a scroom, one barely had to form the question before the scroom sensed it. Grank stared at the scroom of H'rath and a sadness seeped into his gizzard.

Don't be sad, Grank.

It is you, Your Majesty?

Just H'rath. We no longer need titles once gone.

Grank felt himself float and rise toward the limb on which the mist had gathered. And yet when he looked down he saw his body still standing there on the mound.

Have you seen him? Grank thought, but did not actually speak the words.

Yes, he is indeed something to behold.

I am trying, H'rath. Doing all I can to raise him to be a great king like you.

I was a good king, but never a great king. I did not have Ga'.

But he might?

I can't answer....

What can I do for him? If he does have the seeds of great Ga', how can I nourish them?

I am not sure. I have feelings but no real answers....But ... but ... you must urge him to ... Yes! To look for the channels.

Channels? Channels of what?

In the flames, Grank, in the flames.

The mist began to seep away. *H'rath...H'rath...don't leave.*

"Don't leave!" It was his own voice shouting aloud that brought him out of the strange trance. He looked down. He was exactly where he had been: on the mound, his talons firmly digging into the earth. He looked up and blinked where the mist had gathered, where he had floated and spoken to the shape that was H'rath. But there was nothing there. Nothing at all.

CHAPTER EIGHTEEN

At Last, the Beyond

Deep in a cliff cave in Beyond the Beyond, the remaining mates of Dunleavy MacHeath licked the socket where his eye had been. "Hordweard gone, eh?" he said.

"Yes, my lord," a yellowish wolf replied in a tight voice.

"She won't last long without me. Stupid she wolf. She'll come back." He paused. "Won't she?" There was silence. Then his hackles rose and he snarled. "Won't she?" The yellow wolf sank to her knees, lowered the maimed stump of her tail, and said in a quaking voice, "Of course, my lord. Of course!" He rose now and walked slowly about the cave. The newest litter of cubs scattered to the deepest shadows. They already knew not to be in their father's way when he was like this. A tiny black cub named Blackmore had already been kicked so hard by his father that his brains were addled and he stumbled around half the time in a daze. Each of MacHeath's mates had been maimed by him in some way during one of his violent rages. One, Ragwyn, had a terrible scar that ran across her face like a bolt of jagged lightning. Another, Dagmar, had only half her tongue, and Sinfagel, like MacHeath himself, was missing one eye. "Won't she?" He snarled again and again as he walked up to each of his mates. He stood now across from Sinfagel who was groveling at his feet. He nudged her face upward roughly. "Look me in the eye!" He roared and then roared again with laughter. "Quite a pair we make, my one-eyed bonnie! Don't we?"

"Yes, my lord," she answered, terrified.

Three more days passed and still Hordweard had not returned. MacHeath knew that the other wolves had not accepted her into their packs. She was too old for mating, too slow for hunting. "She'll come back. She'll come back," he muttered again and again.

He finally sent Ragwyn to seek her. He wanted at least to know where she was dwelling. Ragwyn returned with more news than he had anticipated.

"She is living close to the cave of Fengo," she told him.

"Does he pay her much attention?" MacHeath asked, suddenly nervous. It would not do to have Fengo taking up with one of his mates. How humiliating that would be! She was still his, by Lupus!

No, no, not really." *Perhaps a bit more than the other wolves,* she thought. But she would not tell MacHeath this. So she moved on to the other news. "Owls have been spotted coming over the southern ridges. They should be here by moonrise."

"You mean Grank?"

"Yes, sir. And two others. Maybe more. I'm not sure."

"Is that so?" MacHeath said slowly. He had never trusted that owl, not in all the years Grank had been coming here. He closed his remaining eye. Sometimes it was almost as if he could still see with his missing eye. It was as if the empty socket had visions of its own of a very private nature. *And what if one of those owls is the one destined to retrieve the ember, the wolf ember?* he thought. Suddenly, MacHeath had an idea. "Ragwyn, get my gnaw-bone." Ragwyn went over to the pile of bones that had been gnawed in such a way as to be inscribed with designs. This was a pastime for many of the wolves, and MacHeath's gnaw-bones were considered crude compared to most others. Still, every wolf leader had his favorite.

"No, not that one, idiot! My best one." He kicked away a pup who had come too close. Ragwyn fetched his best gnaw-bone. It had been scraped and then engraved with a fairly decent profile of one of the volcanoes. "Now listen carefully, Ragwyn. I want you to take this bone to Hordweard and tell her she may keep it if she will provide me with information about the owls." He dropped his voice lower. "Tell her that she can keep the gnaw-bone while she is thinking over my proposition. If she decides to help ... well, let's just say no hard feelings about our little spats — or her leaving."

Ragwyn's eyes opened wide and green with surprise. "Your best gnaw-bone, are you sure?" Before the words were completely out she knew she had made a mistake. He gave her a hard swat across her muzzle, which sent her reeling.

"There he is, lad. There he is." Grank pointed his beak in the direction of a high arching cliff. Fengo had spotted Grank before anyone else and leaped up into the air with excitement, giving howl after howl of joy. As the owls approached, Hoole was mesmerized by the sight of this handsome wolf leaping high into the air, leaping in a stream of moonlight. The wolf's back glinted in the moonlight and bright star-shine that spangled the night. Grank explained that the wolves of the Beyond were not just wolves, but dire wolves — almost three times the size of a normal wolf. As they drew closer, Hoole could see the intense green color of the wolf's eyes. Grank told him about the color, and that deep in Fengo's eyes, one could see something that looked like green fire. And then if

Hoole looked even deeper into the green fire, he might see something else. "It's like the reflection of orange flames from the volcanoes but in the center of that flame, lad, there is a glimmer of blue circled by a shimmer of green, the same green as the wolf's eyes."

"What is it?" Hoole asked.

Grank was evasive. "Oh, maybe nothing. It's different, I imagine, for every creature who looks into Fengo's eyes."

Hoole found this a very unsatisfactory answer. "Does every dire wolf have it?"

"Have what?"

"Have that thing you saw in Fengo's eyes."

"All dire wolves' eyes are green, but none except Fengo's have what I saw."

"Well, why won't you tell me what you imagine it to be?"

"No. That would spoil it for you."

"No, it wouldn't. I promise," Hoole pleaded.

Grank had no intention of telling Hoole that what he had seen in Fengo's eyes so long ago was the ember. The owl ember. Hoole must discover it for himself. Grank had taught Hoole much in the short time he had been on this earth, and the learning would not end, but Grank felt that his role as a teacher was not the same now. He must let Hoole learn things on his own, come to conclusions through his own observations. The time for independent thinking had arrived. Independence would be the best teacher now. So the third or fourth time that Hoole asked the question of what he had seen in Fengo's eyes, Grank simply replied, "End of discussion. Prepare to land and meet my dear friend Fengo."

When his uncle Grank said "end of discussion" he usually meant it. So Hoole kept his beak shut tight.

Fengo welcomed them both. He insisted that all four of them move into his cave. "There are so few trees here, and what ones there are have the most miserable hollows imaginable. Stay here with me. It's comfortable." He gestured to the ledges that protruded from the walls. "Plenty of perches, or if you prefer, nice little owl-sized niches in the walls. That moss on the north wall is very soft."

"That is very kind of you. How would you feel if only Hoole lived with you for the time being?" Hoole swiveled his head quickly toward his uncle, but Grank shot him a sharp glance. Fengo seemed somewhat taken aback.

"Hoole has learned much from me," Grank continued. "But I think it is time for him to . . ." He hesitated. "To move on. There are many different ways of thinking, of living, of behaving. I would like him to come to understand the ways of as many kinds of animals as possible.

Would you take him on for a spell? Perhaps take him on a caribou hunt?"

"Caribou hunt!" echoed Hoole. Now, that sounded exciting! But why was his uncle making him stay with Fengo? Why not Phineas or Theo? He had hoped that he and Phineas might share a hollow — just the two of them together so they could whisper into the day. They had become such fast friends.

After Theo and Phineas and Hoole left to have a quick fly around the ring of volcanoes, Fengo finally found a moment to have a private talk with Grank.

"Let's go inside the cave," Fengo suggested.

"Not to the ridge?" Grank opened his eyes in surprise. That was usually Fengo's favorite place to talk.

"No, too many wolf ears around."

"Spies?"

"Possibly."

When they entered the cave they did not go deep into it, but sat close to the opening with Fengo watching the entry. Lowering his voice, he began to speak. "So what is this visit all about, my friend?"

"Hoole. He's the son of Queen Siv and King H'rath," Grank replied quietly.

"And they are both dead now, I take it?"

"The king died in a tremendous battle on the H'rathghar glacier. His one-time friend and ally Lord Arrin turned on him. Made an alliance with the hagsfiends and swept in. Queen Siv lived. The egg had just been laid before the battle. She was forced to flee with it. But she knew that she could not keep it with her. It was too dangerous. They were hunting her. They desperately wanted the egg."

Fengo got up and paced back and forth several times across the entrance of the cave. "Does the lad know that he is a prince?"

"No. He thinks he was orphaned, or thought so."

"Think? Thought? What do you mean?"

Grank told him how Hoole, unbeknownst to any of them, had met a female gadfeather. He then told him about the attack in the cove and how Hoole was convinced that this gadfeather who helped save him was his mother.

"But you say she flew away."

"Flew away before I had time to really see her. But Hoole is certain that she was his mother."

"And you?"

"I don't know, Fengo. He could be right. The boy has firesight. Did I tell you that?"

"No, as a matter of fact you didn't. Is it as good as yours?"

"Far better. He drains every fire he's around of any image I might see. He had been practicing this during the day when most owls sleep. It's not that he's sneaky in a malicious way. It's just that he has this overwhelming curiosity, and I suppose in some sense he wants to protect me. So he goes off on his own. Taught himself to fish on his own, basically."

"Hmmm, sounds like an interesting lad."

"Oh, he's more than interesting, Fengo."

"You mean he's . . ."

Then Grank cut Fengo off. "Yes, that is precisely what I mean. I believe he's the one, the one who can retrieve the ember and not be overwhelmed by it as I was."

"But how will he learn how to catch coals, colliering? Certainly not from me. I don't understand why you want him to be with me. Not that I object, mind you."

"Oh, he'll learn colliering all right, like he learned how to fly — with little or no instruction. He's a natural. But from you, he can learn the way of the wolves. From you, he can learn compassion for animals different from himself. Had we remained in the N'yrthghar, I would have had him live with a polar bear. I want him to gain empathy with land animals, legged animals."

"It won't be easy. He flies, we run. I don't know whether he'll understand. I can see the lad's quick, but . . ."

"He's more than quick. Anyone can be quick. It's his depth, his feelings for things. The way he reads the telling fires is extraordinary. He doesn't just read them. It's as if he lives them. They radiate within him. That is why I am almost convinced that it was his mother, Siv, that he saw first in the flames and then at the cove. If he lives with you for a while in this cave and smells the scents and breathes the air that you breathe and gnaws the bones that you gnaw, he will begin to sense the real essence of wolves' lives. He will not need to be a wolf. He will become one not in his shape or body but in his mind. And when he travels with you, although he shall be flying, he will feel the fall of every footstep you make as if he is running. His beak will seem like fangs, his feathers like fur. This is his genius. And with his genius, he will learn lessons in compassion that we cannot begin to imagine. I know this, Fengo. He is an extraordinary owl."

CHAPTER NINETEEN
What Hoole Saw

Hoole was fascinated by the new country. He had been sleeping in the cave with Fengo for fourteen days. When they had arrived, the moon had been full but now it was half dwenked. He had adjusted his schedule to Fengo's and often went out with him during the day when he hunted for small game like the cinder shrews that could be found in the warm ashes of the volcano. Or the soot rabbits that hopped about. He would fly overhead while Fengo padded along on the ground. Every night he would ask the wolf when they would be going on a caribou hunt. He was tired of the little scrawny animals that plied their way around the perimeters of the volcano. He was impatient to see the large four-legged animals that were almost the same size as the dire wolves. And most of all, he wanted to see the moose, which were supposed to be immense. Grank called them the polar bears of the Beyond. Fengo's answer was always the same. "You're not quite ready, but soon."

What Fengo meant by "not quite ready" was that Hoole had not yet had a significant fire vision, the vision that would transform his mind if not his body into that of a wolf. It was understandable. The volcanoes had been in their quiescent phase. Only a few small eruptions had occurred. No real flames scorched the sky. Grank, though tempted, resisted making a forge fire, much to Theo's chagrin. Theo entertained himself with trying to pick up the few hot coals that were occasionally spewed from the volcanoes but he did not have the makings of a collier. Grank saw this immediately but did not tell him. Theo was purely a blacksmith. That was his art. Finally, toward the end of the dwenking, the volcanoes became more active. And then by the night when no moon rose or traversed the sky, the volcanoes erupted in a fury that was almost unimaginable.

The owls and the wolf were all on Fengo's favorite mountain ridge. "Look at those flames!" exclaimed Phineas.

"Look at the coals!" Theo said. "They're like thousands of red shooting stars!"

But Fengo and Grank were not looking at any of this. They were watching Hoole. Hoole's amber eyes seemed to grow to twice their normal size. He became very still. *It is like the time when we were on the island*, Grank thought. *He is in some sort of a trance.*

The flames and fires that spewed from the five volcanoes were like no fires Hoole had ever seen before. He did not see the shape of his mother in the flames as he had before. He did not even think of his mother now. He saw wolves, only wolves, and something strange was happening to him. It was almost like the time he went fishing and felt that he had become more fish than owl. First, he felt a mighty heart beating in his chest. And his talons began to change shape. Yet, when he dared looked down for just a split second, he saw the same feet he had always had with their four talons gripping the ridge rocks. He was a Spotted Owl and Spotted Owls did not have ear tufts, but suddenly it felt as if his ear slits were moving to the top of his head and growing into little peaks. His beak began to extend into a squarish muzzle shape. And yet he knew it was still just a beak. And his feathers felt different. He was warmer.

I am not a wolf, but I am a wolf, he thought.

Grank nodded at Fengo. Fengo walked closer to Hoole.

"Hoole, my pup. You are ready to go on the caribou hunt. We leave tonight."

Hoole instantly snapped out of his trance. "I'm ready, yes. I know I am ready."

And so they left on that moonless night when the flames singed the stars, and the coals flew red-hot in the night. They were on a southwesterly course away from the ring of the volcanoes into what Fengo called the high plains. Hoole flew high, directly above Fengo. He could see his wings. He could see the feathers on his legs. If he swiveled his head around he could see his tail. He looked like a normal Spotted Owl. But in his heart, not his gizzard, in his wildly thumping heart, he knew he was a wolf. If he hooted, it would sound to him like a growl or a howl. *I am a wolf.* There were new sensations. One of the strongest was that of smell. He was bombarded by all sorts of strange scents. He realized that he had not rid himself of his body, but somehow entered that of another. Fengo's, he guessed.

As Fengo loped along, other wolves joined him. They were mostly from his pack or clan. They were accustomed to going on hunts like this together. To bring down a caribou or a moose, one could not act alone. The hunt became an elaborate and intricate dance. The wolves numbered almost a dozen. Hoole understood immediately the configuration of the byrrgis, in which his position was in the rear with the males. They were slower than the females, and so the females were in the lead. Even Fengo had begun to fall back when more females joined the pack. Hoole felt himself pressed close between Fengo and Dunmore, a younger wolf who loped with an odd gait due to a crooked hind leg. His heart beat in time with theirs. Long strands of saliva hung from their mouths and although Hoole knew that he had no mouth as they did, nor saliva, he felt the long wet strings blow in the breeze. And the rhythms of the wolves' footfalls became the rhythms of his wing strokes as he flew above them.

He noticed an earless wolf just ahead of him where the females ran. He had seen her before lurking about at the base of the volcanoes. She had seemed apart then. It was as if the other wolves avoided her, but now she was running with this clan. Still, Hoole could feel the tension of the wolves closest to her. *They don't like her*, he thought. Wolves were very playful, always wrestling and nipping at one another, playing games of tag or bone toss, but he realized now that he had never seen this wolf play with any of the other wolves. They never shared food with her, never gave her the slightest friendly cuff. Never spoke to her. So why was she with them now? he wondered. *They distrust her*, he thought. *They are afraid of her in some way.* He knew this as well as he knew anything. But there was something else he knew, and his heart, not his gizzard, went out to her. She was not to be feared at all. He was sure. She had a terrible sadness about her. A terrible unbearable sadness. *Can't they see that? Can't they feel that?*

At dawn, they broke the formation of the byrrgiss to

rest. No caribou had been sighted but they were coming closer to their range. The dry and scrubby hillsides here were riddled with caves. The wolves found a large one and went in. Hoole himself went in, and he wondered if they would notice him. For although he felt totally at ease as a wolf, he knew they would only see him as an owl. But they paid no attention to him. A small hunting team had been sent out to scare up some rabbits or weasels. When they came back, Fengo tore apart the animals they had found and divided the portions according to rank. The earless female, Hordweard was her name, was given the smallest gristliest piece of a rabbit. Even Hoole got a much superior piece, a juicy haunch. Again, no one paid him any heed. He slurped his food just as the wolves did, making loud chomping noises. *Maybe to them I do look like a wolf,* Hoole thought. But when he looked down he saw the same white-spotted breast, the talons, and yet...? It was a mystery.

Hoole did not perch in the cave but settled down, sprawled exactly like the wolves. When he began to edge himself closer to Hordweard, who slept in the farthest corner of the cave, Fengo motioned him away from her. He moved and quickly fell asleep. When he dreamed, he dreamed wolf dreams of running, bursting into attack speed, then slowing and crouching down in tall grass.

Silent signals were given. The wolves slunk down in the thickest part of the grass and pressed their bellies to the ground as they approached the prey. He woke up in the middle of the dream. The wolves around him were stirring, and Fengo was just outside the cave with his muzzle lifted, sniffing the air.

Caribou!

The signal went through the pack. They headed off into the rising sun with their tails slightly raised. The pace was steady. Hoole saw the caribou herd ahead. The herd had speeded up for they were now aware of the wolves. Fengo gave a signal to turn the herd. *Turn them west away from the rising sun. Of course,* Hoole thought, *in a few more minutes the sun would be blinding.*

The wolves increased their speed a bit and four females split off to the north. They streaked up to the flanks of the herd. The rest of the wolves caught up, but then abruptly slowed down. They had positioned the herd where they wanted them, but were not yet ready to attack. Fengo scanned the herd. They were looking for a weak one. One that was old, hungry, or lame. One that could be easily brought down.

They spotted her. She was old and had been running in the middle of the herd but had grown tired and was lagging. As soon as she was several paces behind Fengo, they charged her. Just enough to split her entirely from the rest of the herd. In a surprising burst of speed, the old one took off. Now eight female wolves ran after her in spurts, tiring her out, making her think when they slowed that perhaps they weren't interested. She became confused.

It was like Hoole's dream. He knew exactly what he was to do. Even though he still flew above, he felt part of him descend, crouch in the tall grass, his belly scraping the earth as they approached. The caribou lifted her head. She thought they were gone and became more relaxed. But the stalking had begun in earnest. Closer and closer Hoole crept. He was between Fengo and Dunmore. Fengo lifted his tail. A scent suddenly wafted through the air. He felt the other wolves' hackles raise. Two females darted out and leaped onto the caribou, bringing her down and ripping open a great slash on her neck. She looked stunned but managed to rise to her feet once again. Then three young males charged and tore at her flank.

Blood spurted from all of her wounds. She stood and stared at the retreating attackers. Hoole felt an immense surge of admiration for her, but no pity. She was meat and yet she was more than meat. She was magnificent. Fengo now signaled him. It was their turn. Dunmore, Fengo, and that part of Hoole that had become a creature of earth and not sky, burst out of the grasses. Hoole knew they were coming in for the kill. But still she would not bow. Fengo slowly walked around her, never taking his eyes from hers. She wobbled and then collapsed onto the ground, but she was not dead. Fengo signaled Hoole to come up. And then began the part of the death ritual that Hoole could never have imagined. He saw Fengo bow his head and make all the signs of submissive behavior as if this animal he was about to kill was superior to him in rank, and while he did this, Fengo's eyes and that of the dying caribou locked together. An agreement was being made between predator and prey. It was a moment of great dignity. Something was being agreed upon. Fengo nodded and then sank his fangs into her neck.

"Lochinvyrr" was the wolf word for this odd yet beautiful ritual of death in which the predator respects and recognizes the valor of the dying animal. It would be one of the most valuable and important lessons that Hoole would ever learn.

When Hoole finally returned from the hunt he spent much time alone reflecting on all that he had learned in the time his spirit had become that of a wolf. He thought about the wolves and their strategies, their organization, the way they combined strength and planning; their tactics for traveling, hunting, and sharing food. He would never forget the flawless movements of that chase. He wondered if some of their strategies could be used by owls. He must discuss this with Grank, for although owls and wolves inhabited different realms, why couldn't one learn from the other? He most especially revered the code of lochinvyrr. He had learned all about knightly codes of honor and behavior from Grank but there was nothing quite like lochinvyrr, which honored the prey that was giving up its life so another could live.

But it also seemed to Hoole that the wolves moved through their lives as easily as the stars in the night, as smoothly as the constellations that wheel through the sky. And yet they were deeply superstitious and often distrustful for no reason.

CHAPTER TWENTY
Two Wolves Head North

"I can't believe it!" Theo exclaimed. "You caught a bonk coal on your first try! I've been practicing all summer."

They had been in the Beyond for three cycles of the moon, and when Hoole returned from his hunting trip with Fengo and was completely restored to his old owl self, he began to take more interest in the volcanoes, not so much for their fires but for the coals they spewed forth He had quickly learned how to retrieve the cooler coals that lay on the ground. But it had taken him only one try to catch one of the hottest of coals, the "bonk" ones, that were caught on the fly.

"Look, Theo, I can catch them, but you know what to do with a bonk coal. I am not good at smithing."

This certainly was true. Theo had tried to teach Hoole how to make one of the simplest utensils, a small container that he called a bucket, and Hoole's bucket wound up completely flat and hammered as thin as a leaf. Phineas, trying to be encouraging, said, "Well, it's not that bad. We could use it as a decoration in our cave." The four owls were all living together once again.

Dunmore MacDuncan, to whom Hoole had become very close on the caribou hunt, now trotted up to him.

"Ready for today's lesson?" Dunmore was now in charge of Hoole's education, which focused largely on the activities of the volcanoes.

"I just caught a bonk coal. Isn't that enough for one day?"

"Do you know what a bonk coal sounds like?" Dunmore asked him.

"Sounds like?"

"Ah, so you are in need of a lesson: A bonk coal has a very distinct sound compared to other coals. Now listen."

Hoole crouched down and put his ear slit close to the bonk coal. "It sounds like water! Running water! How can something so hot sound like water?"

Dunmore shrugged. "Don't know. But coals, the lava, the fires of the volcanoes, all have different sounds, and they combine in different ways so that each volcano has a unique sound and even that varies according to weather and certain conditions we don't yet understand."

Dunmore probably knew more about the volcanoes than any other wolf, including Fengo. Fengo had decided to form a guard — a watch — for the volcanoes, and he had made Dunmore the chieftain of the watch. But whenever Hoole asked Fengo or Dunmore why there needed to be a watch, they were evasive in their answers. Hoole sensed that they were watching for something more than just the activity and the sounds and moods of the volcanoes. As Dunmore padded along the perimeter of the ring of volcanoes, and Hoole flew directly above him, he would on occasion stop to point something out.

"You see this one here, Hoole?" Dunmore said. "Listen for a grackling sound."

Hoole hovered. "Grackling? Is that like crackling?"

"Yes, but grittier. It sounds like rocks being broken apart. We think that is just what is happening deep in the volcano — rocks are shattering."

So summer passed and the days grew shorter by slivers of seconds. Grank and Fengo watched Hoole. He had grown into a handsome owl. Both Theo and Phineas, younger and closer to Hoole's age, had been excellent teachers. Theo had shown him rocks that he'd never seen on the island in the Bitter Sea and explained their properties, and which metals could be derived from them.

Phineas had a wisdom beyond his years. In spite of being so small, he had traveled widely, and coming from the Southern Kingdoms, knew every forest there. So soon he was giving Hoole instruction in the immense variety of trees and plants that grew in that unfrozen part of the world. Grank was pleased. The young prince's education had been enriched by these two young owls. And how astounding it had been when Hoole had approached him that night shortly after he had returned from the hunt and told Grank he felt that some of the strategies used by the wolves would work for owls. And then most astonishing were those words he had said in innocent earnestness: "Uncle Grank, if I were king I would make lochinvyrr part of the H'rathian code." It had taken Grank's breath away. *If he were king!*

"Will he see the ember in the way I did?" Grank wondered aloud one night to Fengo where they perched high on their favorite ridge.

"That's unanswerable."

And when he does find it, will it be too late? Grank wondered.

There had been no news from the N'yrthghar about the war since they had reached the Beyond. Grank's fires were unclear as to what was happening. Hoole, oddly enough, did not seem that interested in reading the flames these days. Grank suspected that he was too fearful about his mother, that he did not want to know if she had perished after the encounter with the hagsfiend and Pleek in the Bitter Sea. He never talked about her anymore. But Grank thought of her constantly.

"I wonder what happened to Siv?" he said to Fengo as they perched on the ridge. "How thrilled she would be to see her son now. He truly is becoming a prince."

There was a sudden scrabbling of rock beneath them. Fengo and Grank were immediately alert. They saw the shadow of a wolf dart off in the moonlight.

"Who was that?" Fengo asked nervously. "No one ever comes up here."

But before they could chase the wolf, he had vanished completely.

Neither Fengo nor Grank slept well. Finally, toward noon when the owls usually slept, Grank went out and decided to make a new fire in his forge. As the flames built up, he thought he saw something in them but it was not any image from the N'yrthghar. What he saw was a wolf streaking across the Beyond on an easterly course. The wolf was staying far north on a heading that would take him to the northern edge of the spirit woods, and it looked as if he were heading for Broken Talon Point. This was most unusual. Wolves rarely left the Beyond, and when they did, they usually went south into the Shadow Forest. *Most unusual!* He would monitor the fires and check on the wolf's progress again before he mentioned any of this to Fengo.

The next day when he went to the fires, he blinked in surprise. He saw not only one wolf traveling east and north but two. They were, however, far apart, one seeming to follow the other. That same afternoon, he went into Fengo's cave and roused him from his midday nap.

"What is it?" Fengo's ears rose and twitched. He knew that his old friend would not wake him if it were not important.

"The fires."

"What did you see?" Fengo's green eyes glistened.

"Two wolves heading out of the Beyond, on a course that will take them across to Broken Talon Point."

"And into the Northern Kingdoms — a land route. Longer but easier for a wolf."

"But they'll still have to swim at some point." *Especially,* thought Grank, *if they are heading toward Lord Arrin's stronghold. They will have to cross the Bay of Fangs. Otherwise it would take them years!* "Someone must know that he is here! Great Glaux!" Grank exclaimed. "But what possible interest would it be to the wolves? Who would betray us?"

Fengo was silent. Then stood up. "You go to sleep now, Grank. I'll wake you when I find out more."

Grank, of course, did not sleep and a short time later,

Fengo burst into the cave that he shared with Hoole, Theo, and Phineas.

"I'm sorry to disturb you."

"I wasn't sleeping and I was already disturbed," Grank replied drily. Theo and Phineas, however, had been sleeping. They stirred and blinked. Hoole slept on peacefully, most likely dreaming of bonk coals.

"What's going on?" Phineas asked

"There's a traitor — or two traitors — I should say," Fengo replied gravely. "They are both gone. They are the ones headed toward Broken Talon Point."

"Who?" asked Hoole, who had suddenly awakened.

"MacHeath and Hordweard!" Fengo snarled. "I knew she'd go back to him. I knew she would spy." Fengo was absolutely fuming.

"What's there to spy about?" Hoole asked. Grank and Fengo exchanged nervous looks.

Grank thought quickly. "Well, you know, Hoole — it is rather unusual, owls in the Beyond. And, of course, look at all we are doing here, catching coals, building fires and all sorts of wonderful tools — tongs, containers of all sizes, and that new metal sling that Theo invented. There is much that other owls, particularly those warring in the N'yrthghar, would want to know."

"You mean the bad owls, Lord Arrin's owls?" Hoole

asked. "Not the good owls of the late King H'rath and Queen Siv."

"Yes, precisely, lad," Grank replied.

"And we feel that these two wolves have turned traitor on us. They have learned much and there is always a price for good information," Fengo added.

"Not Hordweard," Hoole said emphatically.

Fengo took a step closer. "What do you mean, 'not Hordweard'?"

"I mean, she's no traitor," Hoole replied in an even voice.

"How would you know this?" Fengo pressed.

"I just know it. I can't explain."

"If you can't explain it, then you shouldn't say it. Nor should we believe it," Fengo said contentiously with a patronizing tone that riled Hoole greatly.

Hoole puffed up his feathers. If he had had ear tufts they would have been sticking straight up. "I know this in the same way that I knew how to hunt caribou like a wolf when I traveled with you. I know this in the way I felt my wings become legs although I still flew. I know this, Fengo. Do not doubt me!"

Grank burned with pride as he listened to Hoole. This was not the whine of a bratty young'un, nor was it the uppity posturing of an ignorant fool. This was an owl whose seeds of Ga' were beginning to stir. There was not a trace of rudeness in his voice. Nor arrogance. This was an owl who knew the truth and felt compelled to speak it regardless of age or rank. This was a *prince*.

CHAPTER TWENTY-ONE

On the Island of Dark Fowl

Siv had flown out of the Bitter Sea direct to Dark Fowl Island. She and Svenka had planned to meet there. It was, at this time of summer, one of the most ice-free places in the N'yrthghar. And therefore safe from hagsfiends. Miraculously, she had not been hurt in the encounter on the island and she could only pray that Hoole had gotten away safely. She was sure they had all escaped because Grank had arrived with two other owls, and both he and the Great Horned Owl were wearing strange-looking claws that appeared as deadly as any ice weapon. But she had seen her son! She had talked to her son!

Svenka's cubs, Anka and Rolf, had grown huge over the summer. They were now as tall as Svenka's belly when she stood up. But they still tumbled about like little cubs. Siv loved watching and playing with them. Berries grew all over the island and they often went berry picking together. They swam beautifully now, like their mother, and were becoming very good at fishing. Siv's gizzard gave a sharp little twinge when she recalled the image of Hoole diving so beautifully into the cove's waters and coming back with a fish, time after time. It was really quite amazing. She had never seen an owl, save for a Fish Owl, dive with such grace and accuracy. He seemed to sense exactly where a fish was going to swim.

She heard frightened yelps from the cubs now.

"What is it?"

"Auntie!" they screeched. Svenka, off seal hunting, was nowhere around.

Siv immediately flew to the nearby point where they had been frolicking in the water. A strange creature was crawling from the sea. She blinked. She could not believe her eyes. It was a wolf! But even wet she had never seen one this enormous. *A dire wolf,* she thought. There was only one place such wolves were known to inhabit — the Beyond. Grank had told her about them. Siv was immediately alert. There was something frightening about this wolf, but she did not want to betray her fear to the cubs. So she drew herself up tall and fluffed out her feathers.

"Greetings!" she said with great dignity.

The wolf grunted something.

"How come you only have one eye?" Rolf asked.

"Rolf, that is very rude," Anka said. "You shouldn't say things like that. Should he, Auntie?"

"You want to know, little one, why I only have one eye?"

Rolf hesitated. "Uh . . . yes." He stole a look at Siv.

Siv's gizzard was roiling. This wolf was setting off all sorts of alarms.

"It's because a very evil wolf bit it out."

"Who was the evil wolf?" Rolf asked.

"Fengo."

Fengo! The name shrieked in Siv's brain. Fengo wasn't evil. Fengo was Grank's best friend. Oh, this was bad. Very bad. She wished Svenka were here. She had to find out what this wolf wanted and send him on his way quickly.

Siv had not spent a lifetime in court without gaining her fair share of diplomatic skills. She knew it was best not to ask direct questions of creatures of whom one was suspect. It only aroused their defenses. So she did not ask where he had come from or where he was going or why. She acted as if it were the most natural thing in the world for a dire wolf from the Beyond to be crawling out of the sea of the N'yrthghar, sodden and exhausted.

"I can tell you are very tired and most likely hungry. Now, what can we offer you? We have some fish and also I have a few lemmings tucked away."

"Thank you, madame," MacHeath said. He enjoyed

her deference, her respect — something his mates rarely showed him. *These owls must know how to train their females better than we wolves do*, he thought.

He found the lemmings quite sumptuous. "Would you like some more?" Siv asked, even though she had only a few left. Wolves, she knew, were known for their very large appetites, much larger than those of owls.

"And how about some of our bingle juice," she offered.

"Bingle juice? I have never heard of that."

"Oh, it's great but if you ..." Rolf began to speak, but Siv shot the cub a sharp glance, and he immediately shut his muzzle. If she could "bingle" this wolf up a little she might get some information from him.

She brought him an ice cup filled with the juice. "The berries for the juice grow all over this island. It is known for the sweetness of its bingle berries."

He took a large swallow of the juice and pronounced it delicious. "I am very tired. I didn't realize the currents would be so strong. I was carried off course."

Should she ask him what his course was? No, she decided. Another cup of bingle juice and it might just come out.

Three cups later, Svenka arrived and the wolf who had introduced himself as MacHeath was somewhat tipsy. His voice had thickened and he was now complaining about his mates. "They give me no respect. No respect at all. Bunch of lazy she wolves is what they be."

"Oh, Svenka, meet our guest. He's from the Southern Kingdoms, Beyond the Beyond." Siv blinked and gave the great polar bear a knowing look. "He had a terrible fight with a wolf named Fengo," she said the word slowly. Siv had told Svenka all about Grank's sojourns into the Beyond. "He says that there are some owls up there now and he is heading north from here but got carried off course by the currents."

Svenka was a quick study. She hid the alarm in her face and greeted him warmly. By this time MacHeath was slurring his words. "I say, all the females of this region are so . . . so . . ." He passed out as he was about to say "so" again.

"Watch him, children!" Svenka said. "Auntie and I have to talk. Tell us if he wakes up."

While MacHeath slept, Svenka and Siv went a short distance away where there was no chance of being overhead.

"He's heading for the Firth of Fangs, I'm sure. And I think he knows about Lord Arrin."

"How can you be sure, Siv?"

"You didn't hear it all. He was rambling on about how

he gets no respect but when a big powerful owl heard what he had to tell him, what he knew, he'd not only get respect, but power. He says there's something in the Beyond — I'm not sure what it is — but he says it's more powerful than anything else on earth. It came out in bits and pieces, and probably not all of it. But he's bad, Svenka. You can see that."

Svenka nodded her huge white head. "I don't doubt you, Siv. I just think we should make sure."

"How do we make sure?" Siv asked.

"I'll follow him. Or better yet, I'll guide him partway to where he wants to go."

"But, Svenka, that could be dangerous for you. Think of your cubs. I know you are strong but the hagsfiends cast their fyngrot on you once. They could do it again."

"Don't worry. I'll take him partway by water. Then I'll show him the overland route, if it is to Lord Arrin's stronghold he wants to go. But I know a shortcut. There are bears up there who are my friends. And remember, at this time of year there is a lot of free water, no ice. We needn't fear hagsfiends. Please don't worry. "

"There's no way I won't worry, Svenka. You know that."

"Yes, I know. But if Lord Arrin finds out that Hoole is in the Beyond . . ."

Siv shuddered at the thought. Svenka was right. Lord

Arrin and his troops had made steady advances against the H'rathian forces that were now scattered and leaderless. If he captured or killed Hoole that would be the end of the N'yrthghar. It would fall under the rule of tyrants and nachtmagen.

"You're right. You must go. Thank you, Svenka."

Later that evening, MacHeath climbed on Svenka's back and the polar bear began swimming across the Everwinter Sea and into the Bay of Fangs. So once more Svenka and Siv parted. Siv perched on Anka's head and the two cubs and the owl waved good-bye.

Meanwhile, an earless wolf took up a post on Broken Talon Point, which jutted into the Southern Sea. Hordweard had followed MacHeath as far as she dared. She knew if he did come back, it would be by this route — and she would be waiting for him. She had become stronger and sleeker on this journey. She hunted for herself now and ate her fill; not subsisting on the scraps left for low-ranking wolves as she had for countless moon cycles. She doubted if she would ever return to the dire wolves in the Beyond. Fengo, for all his brave words that MacHeath's mates could go free, had done nothing to help her. She should have known. No one would go near a wolf once tainted by Dunleavy MacHeath. Wolves and their superstitions! She spat on the ground in disgust. She had become worse than a low-ranking wolf. She had been shunned to the point that she was nonexistent. They looked through her as if she were air. She was invisible to all except for the young owl, the one called Hoole. He had seen her, had even approached her on occasion, only to be warned off by Fengo.

Invisibility had its advantages, however. She would not be missed for a while. When she had finished her business with MacHeath she would go off somewhere. She was not sure where. She would change her name, too. No more MacHeath for her. Her mum's name had been Namara. Perhaps she would call herself that. She would live alone. She needed no one now. She felt younger than she had in years. Hunting for herself, she was better fed than she had ever been. She was limber once again and her coat had grown glossy.

She was unsure what exactly MacHeath was doing, but she was certain that he was up to no good. How furious he had been when she returned the gnaw-bone. In his rage, he flung it at her and missed. It had cracked open on a rock. What a wailing his mates had sent up. Nothing was thought to bode such ill luck as a fractured gnaw-bone. *Superstition again. What fools!*

Still, MacHeath had found out something and was

obviously on his way to the Northern Kingdoms. She sensed that it had something to do with Hoole. She liked Hoole. Something deep within her wanted to protect him, and something even deeper sensed that he was in grave danger. MacHeath had murdered her only pup. She would not let harm come to this young owl. She was sick of MacHeath's bullying and she felt a rage unlike any she had ever experienced. MacHeath would have to come back by the land route. He would be worn out. She would be fresh. Yes, fresh for the kill.

CHAPTER TWENTY-TWO

Svenka's Trek

Grank once again could not sleep. It was nearly autumn, and still Hoole had not discovered nor even sensed the presence of the ember despite frolicking all the livelong night around the volcanoes. Grank and Theo had more bonk coals than they knew what to do with. Grank himself had never seen such a flier as Hoole. He negotiated the fickle hot drafts and vexing cool spots above the craters nimbly and with such grace! Hoole far surpassed Grank's own skills of colliering. He had even taught Phineas and Theo how to catch a few bonk ones, and most extraordinary of all, he had taught some of the wolves on the watch how to jump high and catch coals.

Occasionally, he would ask a few questions of Dunmore about the watch, but he did not seem curious any longer as to what they might be guarding. Had Grank made a mistake about the young'un's destiny? Was Hoole perhaps not the owl he thought he was? A prince by blood, by accident of birth, by name but perhaps not of gizzard?

Perhaps his gizzard was a very ordinary one like most owls in which the seeds of Ga' were lodged but still, doomed never to sprout. But when he remembered that seedling in the middle of the island in the Southern Sea, he took hope. He had not imagined it, for Phineas and Theo had seen it as well. The seedling had grown more in a few hours than most do in a full circle of seasons. They never discussed it. It was as if the strange seedling was a secret that they all kept in their gizzards and that talking about would make less real.

Svenka had left MacHeath just north of the Ice Talons. It would still be a long haul for the wolf to reach Lord Arrin's stronghold. Svenka neglected to tell him that swimming there would be much quicker. Nor did she tell him that she knew an inlet through which she could pass that would get her there a good day before MacHeath would arrive. Once there she planned to find an old friend of hers, Svarr, the father of Anka and Rolf. It was not yet mating season but she knew where Svarr usually denned this time of year. It was not far from Lord Arrin's stronghold. So she climbed out of the sea and headed inland.

"What are you doing here? It's not mating season yet. I'm not really in the mood," Svarr said.

"Don't be ridiculous," Svenka replied. "I'm not here for that."

"What are you here for?" Svarr looked at Svenka blankly.

"Look, Svarr, I know you might have trouble understanding this because ... well ... you're a male polar bear and you don't care really all that much about young'uns and cubs."

"That's for mothers."

"Yes, exactly."

He interrupted before she could continue. "But, by the way, did you have any cubs last season?"

"Yes, three. One died. But the other two are fine."

"Good. Now what is it you've come for?" he asked.

"Well, I've made friends with a lovely female owl. And she is most worried about her young'un. She thinks that Lord Arrin or one of his hagsfiends wants him for some reason."

"Oh, Great Ursa, the way those owls and hagsfiends carry on." Svarr sighed. "This stupid war. Too bad about King H'rath. He was a good bloke. And Lord Arrin's lieutenants are always trying to get young'uns who fought with H'rath to join them. He's a very bad sort."

"Yes, that's just the point. My friend wants to know exactly what Lord Arrin is up to these days." Svenka had to be careful. She didn't want to say too much, but she was actually tempted to tell him a little more. Svarr was a good fellow and she knew that in his own dull way he had really admired H'rath. The only reason Svarr had ventured so close to Lord Arrin's stronghold was that the seal hunting was good.

"Look, Svarr, can you keep a secret?" Svenka asked.

"Who do I ever see, except you once a year?"

"Well, I know sometimes you see what's her name, Svaala?"

"Gone!"

"Oh, too bad."

Svarr shrugged his shoulders. "So, what is the secret?"

Svenka proceeded to tell him that her special friend was Queen Siv. She continued with the story of the young owl prince and the traitorous wolf from the Beyond.

"Your close friend is Siv? My, you've come up in the world."

Svenka was shocked. "How dare you, Svarr! I was up just fine in the world even before I met Siv. Just remember, friends don't make the animal. Animals make friends."

Svarr blinked. *She is pretty smart,* he thought. *Always had a way with words.*

"So do you want me to take out the wolf?" Svarr asked.

"Maybe later, but right now I want to know what that wolf is telling Lord Arrin, and what Lord Arrin is up to. So, I was wondering . . . are there any dried-up smee holes around his place that we could get to?"

Smee holes riddled the N'yrthghar. Some of them dried up over the years and provided snug dens for polar bears. They were known, but only by the bears, to transmit sounds. In the right smee hole one could hear quite clearly a conversation almost a league away.

"Well, as a matter of fact, I know where to find a mess of them."

"Could you take me to one, one that would be especially good to listen to Lord Arrin?"

"Sure, no problem. Too bad it isn't mating season. We wouldn't have to make another trip to meet up."

Svenka rolled her eyes. *Males!* Thank Ursa, one didn't have to live with them all year round.

CHAPTER TWENTY-THREE
Into a Smee Hole

"You say that they call this young owl Hoole?" It was Lord Arrin's voice they were hearing.

"Yes, sir," MacHeath replied.

"And that Grank claimed this Hoole was Siv's chick?"

"Yes, sir," MacHeath said again.

Then Svenka and Svarr heard a collective gasp from the other owls and the hagsfiends in the inner sanctum of the stronghold.

"You know the meaning of this?" A hagsfiend cawed in his ragged voice.

"I know that the first owl was called Hoole and was said to be a mage," Lord Arrin said.

"And not any mage, but a very powerful one," the hagsfiend replied.

"An owl would not be given such a name if it were not thought that he might possess these powers," said the hagsfiend who had spoken first. "It could be the end of all of us."

"We must fly immediately to the Beyond. This owl prince, the one called Hoole whose egg was said to be so luminous, must be destroyed — or he must be ours."

That was all Svenka had to hear. "See you come mating season, Svarr. I have to go."

"Yes, dear."

Svenka ran and then swam as she never had before. She could see Lord Arrin's troops and the hagsfiends rising in the night. She knew that the hagsfiends would not follow the same route as the owls because of all the open water. They, like the wolf, would go due west over the H'rathghar glacier toward Broken Talon Point and then swing south into the Beyond. There was a chance at least that Siv might be able to get there before they did. Svenka knew that she would have gone herself. She could swim all the way to the Southern Kingdoms and then race through the forests, but she couldn't leave the cubs. Not yet at least. *Oh,* she thought for perhaps the thousandth time, *males are so useless. If only Svarr could be trusted to care for them.* It wasn't as if male polar bears were dim-witted, they just seemed to be missing something when it came to feeling any kind of emotion or attachment to anyone but themselves. And yet they could not be called selfish, not willfully so, at least.

Svenka arrived at dawn of the following day.

"You must be exhausted, Svenka," Siv said.

How gracious of her, Svenka thought. *She inquires about me first. So unlike Svarr.* "No, not really. The news is not good. I have confirmed that Hoole is in the Beyond with Grank, and Lord Arrin and the hagsfiends have already set flight."

Siv wilfed until she seemed a quarter her original size. "Oh, dear!"

"The only good news is that the hagsfiends and the wolf are going by the long route because of open water. "

"You mean across the H'rathghar glacier and then west?"

"Yes, it will take them a good while especially with the prevailing winds."

"So I have a chance of getting there before they do."

"Yes, and I don't think Lord Arrin would strike without the hagsfiends. He'll wait for them."

Siv's eyes suddenly brightened. "Svenka, I have one more favor to ask of you."

"Anything, Siv."

"There's a messenger, Joss, who served the king and me faithfully in the past. I suspect that he is in the region of the Ice Talons. The cubs can swim with you there. It is not so far. You can find him. There are usually lots of gad-feathers around there this time of year, one of their many gatherings. Ask around and when you find Joss, tell him that I live and that my son is in mortal danger. That he must quickly gather what troops he can and any hireclaws he can find and fly to the Beyond."

"Yes, madam," Svenka said.

"Madam? Why are you calling me 'madam'?" Siv asked.

Indeed, the word had just slipped out. But when Svenka looked at Siv now she saw not just a regal Spotted Owl of great elegance, she saw an owl of incomparable force and leadership.

"Never mind. But what I was going to say, Siv, is that it is often dangerous to send messages. Other animals can overhear them. I overheard Lord Arrin because of the smee holes."

"I would never send it in plain Krakish. There is a code. It is simple. All you need to say is 'The moon bleeds silver. The ice fox comes before the dwenking.' Do you have that?"

Svenka repeated the code and then she was off, flanked by Anka and Rolf, who were ecstatic to be a part of this adventure.

Siv left immediately, flying first to the Ice Dagger where she had hidden the scimitar of H'rath.

CHAPTER TWENTY-FOUR

A Wolf Waits

Oh, my blood grows hectic and this worm called revenge does twist in my heart and burns out any gentleness, any virtue. I live now only for revenge. Hordweard lay in wait on top of a boulder. So carefully had she covered her tracks with tangled paths of scent marks that any wolf who had wanted to follow her would become hopelessly confused. She wanted no interference, no distractions from her business. And her business was to kill. MacHeath was bound to return this way, if indeed he did return and had not met with trouble. By Lupus, she would not have trouble stealing her revenge!

The sky suddenly darkened above her. She looked up and saw strangely shaped dark birds flying overhead. "Hagsfiends!" she muttered. Although she had never seen one before she had heard of them and knew there could be no mistake. *Yes, of course,* she thought. *And they be flying the wolves' route from the Beyond, for it is water they fear. Oh, that MacHeath has been up to no good.* It had to have something to do with the young owl, Hoole. There was something special about him. Anyone could tell that. Ever since the caribou hunt she knew he had powers. She wondered, briefly, if indeed she should turn back and run to warn them. She liked the young'un. He was the only one who had not shunned her.

But she would not sacrifice the moment that was her due, the moment of revenge. Vengeance was the blood that pumped through her heart, the air she breathed. She loved it with a passion. Vengeance was her mate now, and she would not give it up.

And so she waited. And waited. Never anxious, always patient, polishing her vengeance as if it were a precious thing, gnawing it delicately as if she were etching a bone with her fangs into a magnificent design. *He will come. . . . He will come.* And he did. She smelled him first. *Ah! Even the wind is my accomplice!*

The wind, which had been coming from the west for the last few nights making MacHeath's progress slower, had shifted at last to east. He growled a soft, contented sound of pleasure that at last the wind had turned to help speed his journey. He had anticipated his arrival in the Beyond on the tail feathers of the hagsfiends who by then would have joined Lord Arrin. Finally, MacHeath would be rid of Fengo. A delightful prospect. Yes, Fengo would be killed and his friend Grank and the other owls slaughtered with him. As for his own reward, Lord Arrin had promised him a kingdom. Yes, the Beyond and all the land creatures of the entire Southern Kingdoms would be under his rule. The sky would be Lord Arrin's, but the earth would be MacHeath's — and the volcanoes! He had withheld some vital information from Lord Arrin — that of the ember. Neither Lord Arrin nor the hagsfiends knew of the ember — what nonsense that Fengo had called it the owl's ember. It was the wolf's ember, and with it, by Lupus, he would rule even the hagsfiends.

Hordweard had picked the perfect point from which to observe him. It was a high boulder. Another smaller one perched atop it, perfect for concealing her presence. She saw him coming down the trail. He looked ragged, much thinner. His bones jutted up so that his pelt draped sharply now over the massive shoulders. He breathed hard, too hard for a wolf who was traveling at this easy pace, and she heard a rasping sound in his lungs.

It had begun to snow. The moon had risen and its light fell directly on the boulder. Quietly, she stepped out from behind the boulder. His instincts were off. He did not even hear the scratch of her claws on the rock. She made a low growl. MacHeath stopped, his hackles suddenly stiff, his ears up. He lifted his head. She could see the look of surprise in his one eye. *He does not know it is me,* she thought. *Have I changed that much? As much as he has changed?*

MacHeath blinked his one eye and again was caught in the strange state somewhere between fear and aggression, threat and submission, as his hackles raised and his ears laid back and the odd half-growl, half-whine sound came from deep in his throat.

He actually doesn't recognize me, Hordweard thought. *Have my ears grown back? No!* She knew that this was impossible. *I'll save him from his own confusion,* she thought, and took another step closer to the edge of the boulder.

"It is me, MacHeath."

He stared for a long moment in disbelief. His old mate, the oldest of all his mates suddenly looked young. Her once patchy mud-colored pelt had thickened and turned a tawny gold. She gleamed in the moonlight. Her green eyes, once dull, were now luminous. She was bigger, heavier. He had been gone not quite the cycle of one moon and yet . . . "Hordweard?"

"Yes, but that is no longer my name."

Now his ears and hackles rose even higher. His tail went out straight, and he snarled. "But it is. I name all my mates. You are Hordweard MacHeath!" he snarled.

"No longer MacHeath. I am Namara!"

"You are not Namara, and you have no clan but MacHeath."

"I am a clan unto myself."

Then in the night, there was a golden explosion as she leaped high and howled, "I am Namara! And my clan is MacNamara!"

She hurtled down on top of MacHeath's back. There was the sound of a bone cracking and a terrible howl of pain. He tried to rise but his hind legs flopped out behind him. But still he had his fangs and his front legs with their claws. He managed to roll over and clawed at her chest. He missed but opened a gash on her shoulder. This maddened her.

"I shall not stop till I finish you, MacHeath." She tore at his face. This time he howled not with pain but with unleashed fury and with his broad chest and still mighty shoulders managed to fling her off.

Namara stepped back a few paces. He tried to drag himself toward her. "I'll take your other eye now, MacHeath!"

"No. Never, she wolf from hell." His voice was guttural and raspy with pain and rage.

Although MacHeath's back was broken, his hind legs useless, he still dragged himself toward her. He was dying, she knew it. She had been on enough hunts to know when the end was near. The newly fallen snow had turned red with his blood. She came closer. There was a sudden fear that iced his eye and then a melting, aggrieved look as he finally laid back his ears and twisted his head into a submissive position and exposed his throat for Namara's fangs.

"Namara," he whispered.

He expects lochinvyrr? This cur, this wretched cur expects lochinvyrr?

Namara glared at him now. "You call me Namara, and you expect in return the dignity of lochinvyrr. You cannot give me permission to kill you. I take your life not because it is worthy, not because I respect you, but because I must destroy you!"

"But, Namara — lochinvyrr . . ." MacHeath was gasping now. "Without lochinvyrr I will not find the spirit trail to the star wolf."

"I do not plan to eat you. You now offer up your life to me as if it is something of value. You who have never honored any code now wish for lochinvyrr." Namara laughed harshly. "I'll give you lochinvyrr!" she howled as she raised her forepaw and clawed out his remaining eye. Blood spurted from the socket.

"I am blind, I am blind!" he whispered in despair. The bleeding empty socket flinched in one last desperate attempt to lock his eyeless eyes with his killer.

"You are dead!" she said quietly, and sunk her teeth into his neck.

CHAPTER TWENTY-FIVE

The Scimitar and the Ember

"What's that?" said a tipsy Great Gray Owl as he looked up from his perch on the grog tree.

"Looks like a comet!"

"Naw, ish ish too clossh for a comet," the Great Horned Owl slurred.

An Elf Owl, who had an astounding capacity for bingle juice despite his miniscule proportions, suddenly blurted out, "It's the scimitar of H'rath!"

"His scroom! King H'rath's scroom!" an owl gasped and tipped off his perch plummeting to the ground, recovering just in time.

"It's NOT a scroom!" the Elf Owl shouted. "It's the queen, Queen Siv . . . Queen of the N'yrthghar."

"Oh, Great Glaux," a large Snowy gasped and then belched loudly as Siv settled at the top of the tree. "Your Majesty!" The Snowy attempted a curtsy but sprawled and then only succeeded in hanging upside down on the limb.

Siv held the scimitar high so they could all see it. "Grog seller, cut off the bingle juice. Sober up, all of you!" A sudden silence fell on the tree. *A sorry lot,* she thought, *but they're all I've got to work with.*

"I am no scroom. My husband, good King H'rath, is dead. But we have a son and his name is Hoole," Siv spoke in a firm voice.

"Aaaaaaaah." The sound rolled through the tree.

"I know that many of you here fought with King H'rath and were part of the old H'rathian troops. I am your queen and I now come for your help. The rest of you are perhaps from elsewhere and I am not your queen, but still I ask for your help in fighting for a just cause. Hoole is in danger now, grave danger. Lord Arrin and an elite unit of hagsfiends are flying this way and on to Beyond the Beyond, where they plan to destroy young Hoole, heir to King H'rath." There were more gasps.

"The hagsfiends are coming to the Southern Kingdoms?" a Burrowing Owl asked.

"Yes. This is the brutal truth. Furthermore, Lord Arrin has made significant advances in the N'rythghar. He is within striking distance of capturing the Glacier Palace. We are losing the war, and we shall definitely lose if he captures or kills young Prince Hoole. I know you owls of the Southern Kingdoms. You are good owls. You feel with your gizzards and think with your brains. You are compassionate, smart owls and would never rely on the cheap yet deadly art of nachtmagen that has beguiled so many. Together, we stand for decency, compassion, and honor. So I ask now who will join me in the fight — this battle that is a battle against tyranny, a war against nachtmagen. This a war to save the very soul of owlkind."

"I will! . . . We will! . . . Hail," a huge cry went up. "Siv, our queen, lives. Our queen lives!" Never had the grog seller seen so many of his customers sober up so quickly.

The news that the queen was alive swept through the forests of Tyto, of Silverveil, of the Shadows, Ambala, and even as far as the Desert of Kuneer. With the scimitar of H'rath clutched in her talons, Siv led a ragtag company of veteran owls made up of hireclaws and finally the H'rathian troops, which Joss had gathered as soon as he received word from Svenka. Joss and an old lieutenant, Lord Rathnik, flanked her on either side, protecting her from adverse winds and making her flight easier. But she steadfastly refused to have any owl fly in front of her, which would have eased her flight considerably. She knew that no leader worth her gizzard went into battle anyplace but in the front line. And on her tail flew none other than the Snow Rose, who had given up her gadfeather ways for a short time and joined the order of the Glauxian

Sisters. She soon found that meditation was not a vocation for her. So when she heard of Siv's mission she decided that the time had come to put aside meditation, wandering, and singing alike, and she set forth. For years, she had flown hither and yon not knowing precisely why or where she was going. So she joined a group heading south and when they met up with the swelling troops heading for the Beyond, she nearly staggered in flight, in a manner most embarrassing for a former gadfeather, when she discovered that their leader, Queen Siv, was in fact her old friend Elka!

They flew fast on a route that Joss was certain would avoid an encounter with Lord Arrin. They entered the Beyond at dawn and then flew to the ring of volcanoes where Siv knew Grank and Fengo often stayed. She asked that the hireclaws and the H'rathian troops except for one unit, the Ice Regiment of H'rath, wait behind. She wanted to greet her son and Grank alone and to prepare them with her news.

As she approached the volcanoes, she gasped. It was twilight, or tween time as owls called it, that time between the last drop of the day's sun and the first shadows of the night, but never in her life had she seen such a beautiful tween time. The sky was beginning to purple as the sun sank beneath the horizon and soaring up against the purple of the sky were the fiery reds and oranges of the volcanoes' flames. All five were now erupting. And between the towering flames a lone owl flew, flew so magnificently it took her breath away. "It's Hoole," she whispered to herself. His face was aglow as he caught one bonk coal after another.

CHAPTER TWENTY-SIX
The Ember Beckons

Hoole saw her at the same time Grank did. They both flew to her. Then in mid-flight, Hoole shouted, "Mother!"

"Yes, my dear," Siv replied as all three lighted down in the cinder beds near Fengo's cave.

"Mother," he repeated softly, then turned to Grank. "Why did you never tell me?"

Siv spoke: "He had good reason, dear, and there is no time to explain now. I have come to warn you. Any hour, Lord Arrin, his forces, and the hagsfiends will arrive."

"They know he is here?" Grank asked.

"Hordweard!" Fengo said. "I knew it."

"No, not Hordweard!" Hoole said firmly. And just at that moment, they heard a commotion among the wolves. Dunmore MacDuncan came up.

"Sir, a most unusual . . ." He paused, then continued. "Unusual event."

"What's that?"

"Oh, Glaux, not yet the hagsfiends." There was deep anguish in Grank's voice.

"No. It is Hordweard. She is back."

They all turned and saw the wolf much transformed. But it was definitely Hordweard, and she was dragging the body of Dunleavy MacHeath.

"I told you she wasn't a traitor!" Hoole lofted himself joyously up and down into the air.

"Oh, no," Siv said. "It is the dead wolf who was the traitor."

Hordweard dropped the body at Fengo's paws. "I know not what he told Lord Arrin," she said, "but I fear it was something to do with young Hoole. I should have killed him before he went there but I was not strong enough then, not big enough, not nourished enough." She slid her green eyes around to look at the rest of the wolves who had gathered, including the nervous mates of MacHeath. "One must be well fed and strong to kill a tyrant such as Dunleavy MacHeath."

"Hordweard," Fengo began, and laid back his ears. The other wolves looked on in awe. Never had they seen Fengo even begin these motions of submission. But he now crouched down and drew his lips back. His tail was low. "Hordweard," he began again.

"Fengo, my name is no longer Hordweard MacHeath. I am Namara MacNamara."

"Namara MacNamara, I ask you to forgive my most . . ." He hesitated. "My most uncivilized behavior. I thought at first that it was a grand gesture I made when I said that the mates of MacHeath were free to leave his clan. I now realize it was nothing more than a gesture, and I did not have the will to trust such a brave wolf as yourself. I ask for your forgiveness."

"I forgive you, Fengo."

Just at that moment all the wolves began to howl in alarm. Overhead, the sky darkened as an advanced guard of hagsfiends flew across the flame-torn sky.

"Krakia H'rath Regna Vinca," Siv bellowed the command in Krakish that summoned her troops.

"Quick, battle claws!" Grank ordered. There were only four sets of the claws, but Siv's troops had come armed with all manner of weapons. The H'rathian units had their deep ice weapons and the hireclaws carried sharp branches and their own finely honed talons, which they took pride in sharpening daily on flint stone. Just before they took off, Grank remembered his encounter with the scroom of H'rath. "Hoole, look for the channels!"

Hoole blinked. The channels, yes he knew the channels, the cooler paths through the flames. He hadn't known that Grank did. "Yes, Grank, the channels!" And he rose into the air.

Soon the sky was seething with owls and hagsfiends. The hagsfiends seemed to gain power from the fire and yet they often staggered in flight between the sudden updraft of hot air and the swirling whirlpools of cool air. Lord Arrin's troops were having real trouble flying, and Hoole with his battle claws delivered a fatal blow to a Snowy Owl in Lord Arrin's elite guard.

"Stay close, Hoole," Siv flew up to him and whispered.

"I can fight for myself, Mother."

"I know, son, but if the fyngrot is cast . . ." She saw the Snow Rose and Grank begin to chase down a hagsfiend. If they could attack from the rear they could avoid the fyngrot. But Glaux help them if it wheeled around. Hoole quickly saw how this strategy would work. His lessons of hunting with the wolves came back to him.

"Mother, Phineas, Theo, follow me." They would make a flying byrrgis and use the same strategies to bring down a hagsfiend. *Yes, look for the channels!* And no one knew these channels as well as Hoole. There was one that he called the "river" for it seemed to flow just like a river. And during the most violent eruptions, like the ones that were now occurring, this "river" became as tumultuous as white-water rapids. The currents dumped downward directly into the mouth of the volcano. For the unsuspecting, it was a true death trap, but if one was ready, it was possible to ride it out and peel off in the nick of time. Could his mother with her crippled wing survive the ride? He couldn't take the chance. Instead of leading the hagsfiends toward the channels, they would have to drive them from behind. He slowed his flight so his mother, Theo, and Phineas could catch up. Quickly, he told them the strategy. "Mum, stay close by. The idea is to push them from behind toward the channels."

The four owls then swept down on a trio of hagsfiends, and Hoole immediately started driving them toward the nearest channel that fed into the cool river of air. Theo and Phineas kept up a flanking pressure on either side of the trio. The hagsfiends wobbled in flight as soon as they hit the coolness and then they were swept into the river. They panicked utterly as they spun out of control.

First one, then another, fell into the crater of boiling lava.

"Port wing! Hoole, port wing," his mother called out frantically.

Hoole felt his gizzard seize up. There was a terrible hagsfiend flying right toward him now. A strange yellow glare emanated from his eyes. They were not in a cool spot but an intensely heated updraft. He could not stop staring at the fyngrot. He felt it tightening around him, strangling him. He began to reel. His wings would not work. Suddenly, a shadow passed between him and the fyngrot. It was the shadow of an owl with a misshapen wing.

"Mum, what are you doing?"

"Hold steady, my prince. Hold steady."

Twice before, Siv had resisted the fyngrot, become completely impenetrable to its effects. The first time was in the Ice Cliff Palace when the hagsfiends had tried to steal the egg she had just laid. The second time was when they had brought her to ground on an ice floe. She had resisted by sheer will and the most intense concentration imaginable. She had focused on the scimitar of her noble mate the king, and she would do the same now. But this time she had two images in her mind's eye — that of her mate and that of her son. The king and their prince. And Hoole watched as his extraordinary mother beat back the fyngrot, her scimitar raised and slashing through the yellow light.

Hoole felt his own gizzard begin to unlock. The yellow seemed to be receding. The hagsfiend began to look quite ordinary to Hoole. The hagsfiends themselves seemed to sense how ordinary they had become to both Hoole and Siv.

Fengo perched on his ridge, his claws digging into the dirt as he watched the battle. Red missiles from the eruptions scoured the sky while yellow flashes of the fyngrot soaked up great patches of darkness. Lord Rathnik, leading the Ice Regiment of H'rath, flew high above the flames. Their ice swords and daggers sparkled red in the reflections of the flames as Lord Arrin and his troops swarmed in to meet them. Below, the wolves howled their mad songs, and above, ragged clouds raced across the moon. It was a scene straight out of hagsmire, and the hagsfiends, drunk with the taste of blood, hoisted the heads of slain owls on their pikes in ghoulish delight.

Hoole heard the Snow Rose shriek but paid no heed. From the corner of his eye he saw a splash of blood in the night. But there was something else that drew his attention more strongly. His gizzard began to tingle in a way he had never experienced. He felt as if he were being drawn, inexorably drawn, toward something wonderful. He flew toward a volcano that they had begun to call Dunmore and dissolved through a rip in a wall of flames. The din and the chaos of war seemed to have been left behind him. He was alone now flying over the crater of Dunmore and in the center of the crater he saw something sparkling as fiercely as a wolf's green eye. But soon he realized that in the center of the flame was a lick of blue ringed by green.

It was an ember floating in a cradle of lava. The sides of the volcano were beginning to turn transparent, and he could see the gleaming brilliance of this ember shining through it, turning the entire volcano a shimmering green with splashes of orange and blue. The grackling of the boiling lava seemed to grow still, the closer he flew. The ember beckoned him.

Below, a curious silence had descended on all. The warring owls flew to ground behind their battle lines, and even the hagsfiends remained still and unmoving. Grank was awash in grief as he held the dying body of his queen. Dunmore whispered to him: "He has found it, Grank. Listen to the volcano. He has found it."

Suddenly, Hoole burst through the wall of flames with the ember clutched in his beak, his feathers slightly singed, and a splattering of lava on his talons. A beautiful radiance seemed to pour from the ember and bathe Hoole's face. Indeed, his entire body was enveloped in a shimmering cocoon of light. And above Hoole's head a sparkling crown hovered as if the very stars from the sky had descended to anoint this prince who was now a king.

"Hail, Hoole, son of King H'rath, son of Queen Siv!" A murmur swept through the gathered owls and wolves. The wolves began to crouch to their knees and lay back their ears. Then Lord Rathnik and the noble knights of the Ice Regiment of H'rath kneeled and took up the cry. "Hail, Hoole, King of the N'yrthghar." The wolves howled and the owls hooted and hooted. But in the background almost as loud as the cheering was the low roar of wings flapping. The hagsfiends were leaving. Lord Arrin's troops were in complete disarray. Some fled with the hagsfiends. Others fell to their knees and began to hail the new king. Lord Arrin could be heard screeching, "But he is just a boy. There is no proof of his parentage. He is an unknown, barely fledged owlet. Not even a prince."

Hoole set the ember down between his two feet. "A prince?" He blinked in complete bewilderment. "My mother, a queen?" And then he caught sight of Grank holding his mother's bleeding body.

"Mother!" He flew over to her.

"What they say is true, Hoole," Siv said.

"Mother, don't talk now. You are wounded."

"I am dying, Hoole."

"No! No! You can't be dying."

"I am, but fear not. My life is complete. I feel only happiness, my son, my prince, my king," she whispered faintly and died.

Grank gently shut her eyes with his beak. He felt his heart crack open, his gizzard wither.

"I only wanted to be her son a little bit longer," Hoole said in a hushed voice to Grank.

"You will always be her son, Your Grace. But you are now our king."

After several long minutes, Hoole straightened up and turned to look at the masses of owls and wolves still on their knees.

"Please rise, all of you," he commanded, and then he flew a short distance to that noble knight Lord Rathnik. Before him he knelt and if he had had ear tufts he would have laid them back. The owls and wolves grew still again. "Lord Rathnik, I have heard of your noble deeds in both war and peace from Grank, my foster father and tutor. Before I become a king I must become a knight. I am not sure if I have yet fought long enough or valiantly enough to be worthy of such a title."

"Oh, indeed you have, Your Grace." The Whiskered Screech touched him on his shoulders with his ice sword and dubbed him a knight. "In the name of Glaux and of your good father, King H'rath, and your good mother, Queen Siv, I dub thee a knight of the H'rathian Guard of the Ice Regiment."

Hoole then rose and turned to the multitude of owls. "Who was it who slew my mother the queen?" There was a sudden rustling on a distant ridge and a clutch of owls rose up and sped off into the night. In the middle of those owls was Lord Arrin.

"A cowardly retreat this lord does make," Hoole muttered.

He turned and looked at the lifeless body of his mother.

"You will see her again when you leave this world, dear Hoole," Grank spoke softly.

"In glaumora," Hoole said and then flew over and bent down to touch his mother's lovely face with his beak. "In glaumora."

CHAPTER TWENTY-SEVEN
Into a New Night

The Golden Talons glowed in the sky directly over the crater of Dunmore. The owls had gathered on the ridge along with Fengo and Namara and several other wolves.

"So," Fengo said, "it is time for you to go, eh?"

"Yes." Hoole nodded. "How can I ever thank you for the lessons I have learned from you? Forgive my sometimes impudence."

"It was not impudence. It was the truth," Fengo replied, glancing at Namara. "And where shall you go — back to the N'yrthghar?"

Lord Rathnik took a step forward. "I am afraid there is no longer a palace for our king, nor a throne. It fell to the hagsfiends and Lord Arrin in the last battle of the H'rathghar glacier."

"No matter," Hoole said quietly. "I need no palace of ice nor a crown to be a good king. I need only a code of honor and a gizzard of good grace." Hoole looked to the east where the sun would rise in several hours. "There is an island in that vast boisterous sea of the Southern Kingdoms, and I think that Grank and Theo, Phineas, and Lord Rathnik and his knights of the Ice Regiment of H'rath will fly there with me. The island draws me. It is a special island, I think, with a special tree. And it is there that I shall have my court."

"Well, Glaux speed you, Hoole," Fengo said.

"Yes." Namara came up to Hoole and laid back her ears.

"No. No, Namara. Stand tall and wish me well."

"Glaux speed," the golden wolf said with a tear in her eye.

And so the owls rose in that star-scattered night and headed east toward the sea, and as dawn lightened the horizon they could see the crown of an immense tree breaking through the clouds that raced above the layers of fog. As the fog cleared away, Grank gasped when he caught sight of this island and its magnificent tree. The tree glowed as luminous as that egg he had taken so long before to nurture and raise on another island in another sea. That island had had no name, nor did this one. He wondered what it might be called. And as if reading his thoughts, Hoole said, "Look! Just look at that island and the tree! What should we call it?"

This is a good tree. . . . It has . . . Ga', Uncle Grank. Yes, Ga'. Hoole's words suddenly came back to Grank. He swiveled his head toward the young king. "You said the tree had Ga', lad. We should call it Ga'Hoole. Ga'Hoole," he shouted to the clouds and to the rising sun.

The dozen owls flying with them took up the cheer and shouted it to the world: "Ga'Hoole!"

So ends this story of Hoole forged in the fires of my memory.

Epilogue

Coryn closed the book and looked at his uncle Soren. "He was so noble! Oh, that I might be as noble."

"You will," Soren said quickly. Digger, Gylfie, Twilight, and Otulissa all nodded.

"Forged in the fires of his memory," Otulissa said softly. "I think it was Theo who wrote this down. Theo, the first blacksmith."

"But what is the meaning of it all?" Digger asked. "Why did Ezylryb want you to read this?"

Otulissa answered quickly. "To instill in all of us those ancient codes of honor, of trust."

"Perhaps," Digger, the most philosophical of all the owls, said slowly. "But there is something beyond that."

Otulissa began to interrupt with another theory.

"Quiet, Otulissa," Soren said. "Let Digger speak."

"The ember has great powers, powers that we know that Nyra desperately wanted. But did she want them just for herself?"

"I think not," Coryn said. He paused a long time. He

could not bring himself to tell the others what Soren already knew. That he suspected his own mother was a hagsfiend. "I know," he continued, "that there are still some hagsfiends that fly about, but they are weak and impotent. They skulk around the edges of the night and are easily dispersed like fog on a sunny day. I know because I have encountered them. But now that the ember is back, they could gain power, especially with Nyra as their leader."

Soren now spoke. "Before Ezylryb died, he warned us of the power of the ember."

"Perhaps," said Gylfie, "the final legend will tell us more."

"Perhaps," replied Coryn. He spoke slowly with great reflection. "It is as if for centuries we have lived in a blessed world. Yes, we have had our battles, our enemies. Yes, there were flecks that could destroy owls' minds and will, but there was no nachtmagen. We have lived in a world of reason, not magic and spells. But now it is as if the fragile, invisible membrane that has sealed off our world so long from the irrationality of spells and charms has been torn — and through that small tear . . ." Coryn's dark eyes grew huge and darker. He swiveled his head around to look at each one of these owls. "Through this small tear, I fear nachtmagen is once again seeping into the Glaux-blessed world of owls."

OWLS
and others
from the

GUARDIANS *of* GA'HOOLE SERIES

The Band

SOREN: Barn Owl, *Tyto alba*, from the Forest Kingdom of Tyto; escaped from St. Aegolius Academy for Orphaned Owls; a Guardian at the Great Ga'Hoole Tree

GYLFIE: Elf Owl, *Micrathene whitneyi*, from the Desert Kingdom of Kuneer; escaped from St. Aegolius Academy for Orphaned Owls; Soren's best friend; a Guardian at the Great Ga'Hoole Tree

TWILIGHT: Great Gray Owl, *Strix nebulosa*, free flier; orphaned within hours of hatching; a Guardian at the Great Ga'Hoole Tree

DIGGER: Burrowing Owl, *Athene cunicularia*, from the Desert Kingdom of Kuneer; lost in the desert after an attack in which his brother was killed by owls from St. Aegolius; a Guardian at the Great Ga'Hoole Tree

The Leaders of the Great Ga'Hoole Tree

CORYN: Barn Owl, *Tyto alba*, the new young king of the great tree; son of Nyra, leader of the Pure Ones

EZYLRYB: Whiskered Screech Owl, *Otus trichopsis*, the wise old weather-interpretation and colliering ryb (teacher) at the Great Ga'Hoole Tree; Soren's mentor (also known as LYZE OF KIEL)

Others at the Great Ga'Hoole Tree

OTULISSA: Spotted Owl, *Strix occidentalis*, a student of prestigious lineage at the Great Ga'Hoole Tree

OCTAVIA: Kielian snake, nest-maid for Madame Plonk and Ezylryb (also known as BRIGID)

Characters from the Time of the Legends

GRANK: Spotted Owl, *Strix occidentalis*, the first collier; friend to King H'rath and Queen Siv during their youth; first owl to find the ember

H'RATH: Spotted Owl, *Strix occidentalis*, King of the N'yrthghar, a frigid region known in later times as the Northern Kingdoms; father of Hoole

SIV: Spotted Owl, *Strix occidentalis*, mate of H'rath and Queen of the N'yrthghar, a frigid region known in later times as the Northern Kingdoms; mother of Hoole

MYRRTHE: Snowy Owl, *Nyctea scandiaca*, faithful servant of Queen Siv, formerly her nursemaid and governess; flees with Queen Siv after the death of H'rath

RORKNA: Spotted Owl, *Strix occidentalis*, Glauxess of the Glauxian Sisters' Retreat on the Island of Elsemere; cousin of Queen Siv

LORD ARRIN: Spotted Owl, *Strix occidentalis*, traitorous chieftain of a kingdom bordering King H'rath's realm; killed H'rath

PLEEK: Great Horned Owl, *Bubo virginianus*, enemy of King H'rath; known to consort with hagsfiends and to have taken one, Ygryk, for a mate

THEO: Great Horned Owl, *Bubo virginianus*, a gizzard-resister and apprentice to Grank; possesses great blacksmithing skills

SVENKA: Polar bear in the Bitter Sea; comes to the aid of Queen Siv

SVARR: Polar bear, father of Svenka's cubs

PENRYCK: Male hagsfiend, ally of Lord Arrin

YGRYK: Female hagsfiend, Pleek's mate

KREETH: Female hagsfiend with strong powers of nacht-magen; friend of Ygryk

ULLRYCK: Female hagsfiend, deadly assassin in Lord Arrin's service

BERWYCK: Boreal Owl, *Aegolius funereus*, a member of the Glauxian Brothers and friend to Hoole and Grank

PHINEAS: Northern Pygmy Owl, *Glaucidium californicum*, friend of Hoole and owl of great pluck

THE SNOW ROSE: Snowy Owl, *Nyctea scandiaca*, gadfeather and renowned singer

FENGO: dire wolf, chief of all the clans; friend of Grank

DUNLEAVY MACHEATH: dire wolf, leader of the MacHeath clan, and enemy of Fengo

HORDWEARD: dire wolf, former member of MacHeath clan and former mate of Dunleavy MacHeath; also known as Namara MacNamara

Coming soon!

GUARDIANS OF GA'HOOLE

BOOK ELEVEN

To Be a King

by Kathryn Lasky

One final legend remains in Ezylryb's secret library. In its ancient pages, Soren, Coryn, Otulissa, and the Band find a time in which nachtmagen rages through the N'yrthghar and hagsfiends and traitorous lords conspire to defeat Hoole, the new king.

With Grank and Theo at his side, Hoole must forge an army of free owls strong enough to defeat the forces of darkness massing on the horizon. He vows to avenge his father's murder. The power of the owl ember fires the young king's gizzard and he achieves greatness. But for Hoole there is a danger much closer — and much greater — than the treachery of old allies and the poison of half-hags. For the lure of magic — even good magic — brings great peril to those who would wield it.

About the Author

KATHRYN LASKY has had a long fascination with owls. Several years ago, she began doing extensive research about these birds and their behaviors — what they eat, how they fly, how they build or find their nests. She thought that she would someday write a nonfiction book about owls illustrated with photographs by her husband, Christopher Knight. She realized, though, that this would be difficult since owls are nocturnal creatures, shy and hard to find. So she decided to write a fantasy about a world of owls. But even though it is an imaginary world in which owls can speak, think, and dream, she wanted to include as much of their natural history as she could.

Kathryn Lasky has written many books, both fiction and nonfiction. She has collaborated with her husband on nonfiction books such as *Sugaring Time*, for which she won a Newbery Honor; *The Most Beautiful Roof in the World*; and most recently, *Interrupted Journey: Saving Endangered Sea Turtles*. Among her fiction books are *The Night Journey*, a winner of the National Jewish Book Award; *Beyond the Burning Time*, an ALA Best Book for Young Adults; *True*

North; A Journey to the New World; Dreams in the Golden Country; and *Porkenstein*. She has written for the My Name Is America series *The Journal of Augustus Pelletier: The Lewis and Clark Expedition, 1804* and several books for The Royal Diary series including *Elizabeth I: Red Rose of the House of Tudor, England, 1544* and *Jahanara, Princess of Princesses, India, 1627.* She has also received The Boston Globe Horn Book Award as well as The Washington Post Children's Book Guild Award for her contribution to nonfiction.

Lasky and her husband live in Cambridge, Massachusetts.

Out of the darkness a hero will rise.

The soaring finale to the Legends trilogy!

Coming Fall 2006

*O*nce Hoole reclaims his father's throne, he goes to war against the powerful warlord-tyrants. Grank aids his king by forging weapons for the fight. With great trepidation, Hoole must decide whether using the power of the Ember in the ultimate battle will end the war and bring peace—or destroy the kingdom.

■SCHOLASTIC

www.scholastic.com

GG11T

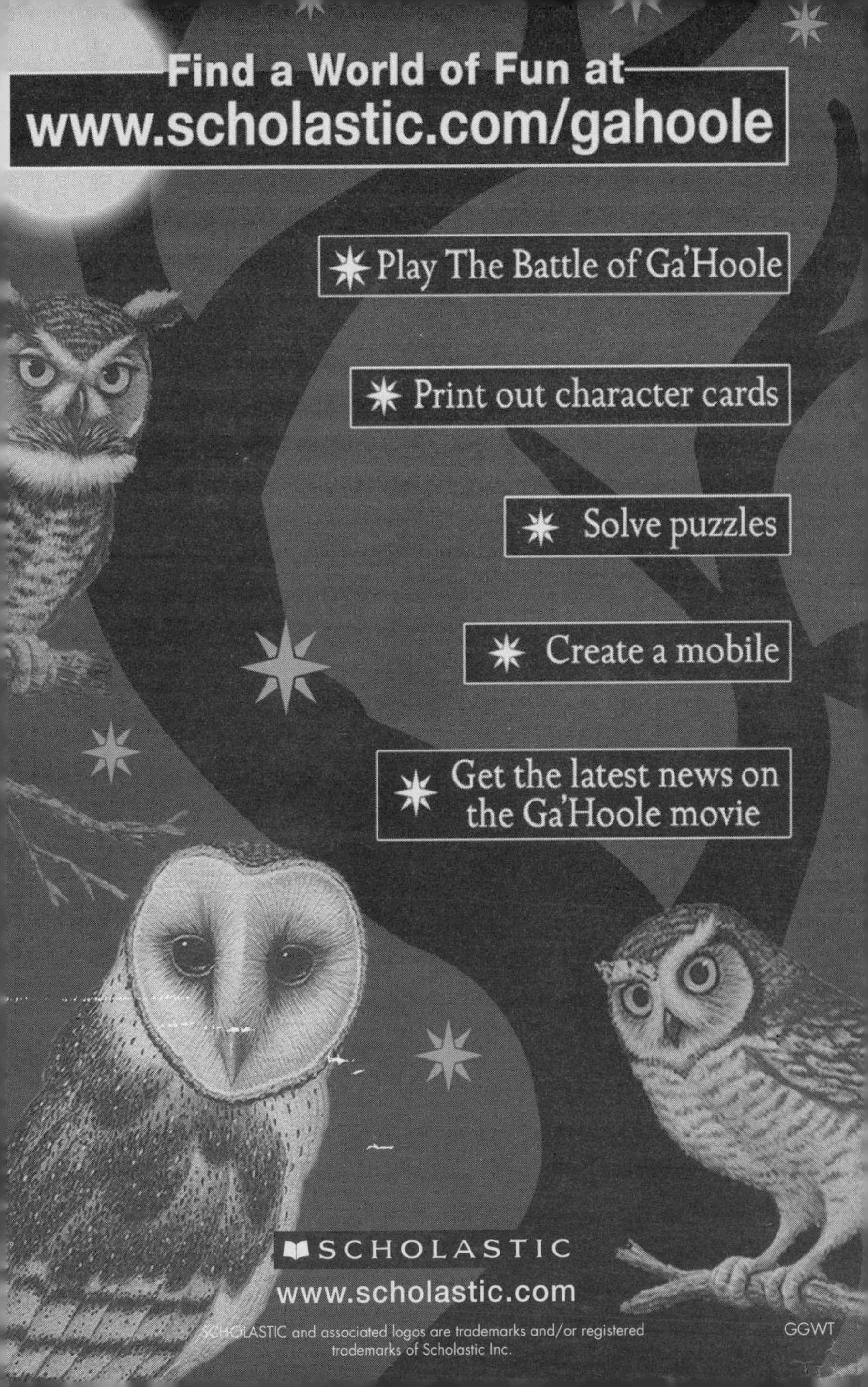
Find a World of Fun at
www.scholastic.com/gahoole
Play The Battle of Ga'Hoole
Print out character cards
Solve puzzles
Create a mobile
Get the latest news on the Ga'Hoole movie
SCHOLASTIC
www.scholastic.com
SCHOLASTIC and associated logos are trademarks and/or registered trademarks of Scholastic Inc.
GGWT

As Night Falls, a Dark and Deadly Force Comes to Life

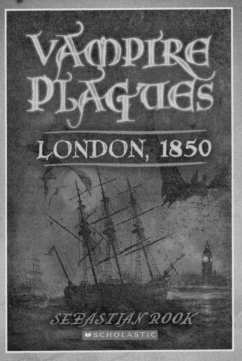

Jack Harkett thinks he is the only one who has witnessed a ghost ship sail into the harbor and release its deadly cargo: a black cloud of bats. Until he meets a boy— the ship's sole survivor—who tells Jack about the vampire plague that killed the ship's crew… and is about to attack London.

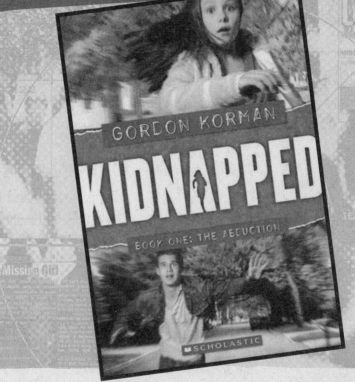

THE SEARCH IS ON!

GORDON KORMAN

KIDNAPPED

BOOK ONE: THE ABDUCTION

SCHOLASTIC

The action never stops in this new adventure trilogy from the author of Dive, Island, and Everest. When his sister Meg is abducted right in front of his eyes, Aiden has three questions:

WHERE IS SHE? WHO TOOK HER? AND WHY?

SCHOLASTIC

WWW.SCHOLASTIC.COM